The Carpenter

by Tim Snyder

This book is dedicated to my grandfather, Cecil Goodfellow –the first of many carpenters in my life.

###

The events in this story took place between 2006 and 2014. All characters are fictional.

###

PART 1

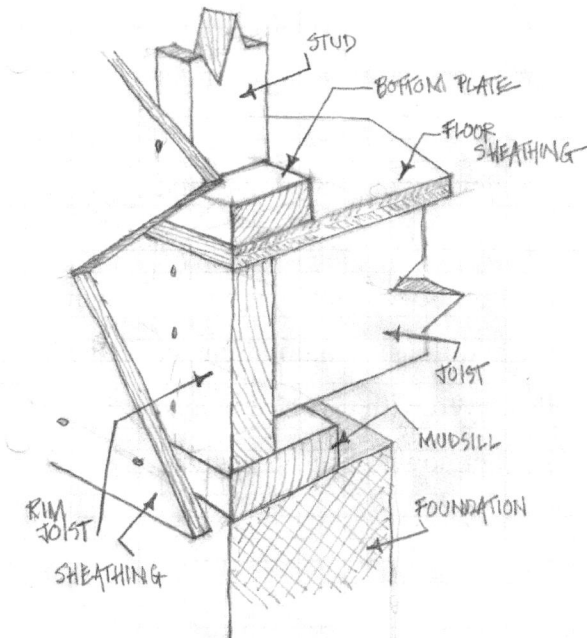

STUD
BOTTOM PLATE
FLOOR SHEATHING
JOIST
MUDSILL
FOUNDATION
RIM JOIST
SHEATHING

Foundation

the basis or groundwork of anything: the moral **foundation** of both society and religion. (CONSTRUCTION) the natural or prepared ground or base on which some structure rests. the lowest division of a building, wall, or the like, usually of masonry and partly or wholly below the surface of the ground.

Chapter 1

Rafters and studs. Baseboard and crown. Soffit vents, stair stringers, joists, headers, drywall, cement board. I learned the language of construction at an early age. It was my dad's business. For the most part, he took on remodeling and home repair jobs in and around our small town in central Connecticut. New construction projects only came along once in a while, mostly in the form of home additions, or outbuildings like sheds and garages. While other kids played with toys, I was unspooling my dad's tape measure, figuring out how to use a try square, and fooling around with levels and chalk lines. More than anything, I was fascinated with all the noisy, dangerous power tools he used for different cutting and drilling jobs.

I know my dad was pleased about my interest in his work. But the time we spent together in his workshop or on jobsites often came about through necessity rather than by choice. My mom went back to school when I was 10, majoring in English and education in hopes of becoming a high school teacher. Part of my dad's supporting role was to look after me when I wasn't in school or hanging out at a friend's house. There were many days when he'd pick me up after school and take me along to a remodeling project. In the beginning, there were crayons and coloring books in the glove compartment of his truck to keep me occupied, along with a small bag of plastic soldiers stowed behind the seat. But these toys couldn't compete with my dad's arsenal of tools –all the functions they performed and the different noises they made. The high-pitched whine of the chopsaw, the impact driver's staccato machine gun impersonation, the intermittent chugging of the air compressor, with accompanying shots from the nail gun. I think any kid would have left toys behind to take part in the magic of making things.

My carpentry apprenticeship started with simple lessons, like the importance of keeping a jobsite clean and well organized. I learned about protecting a work area with drop cloths, and coiling up the long extension cords my dad used on a regular basis. The shop vacuum was the first power tool I was allowed to use –much less dangerous than circ saws and routers. It felt great to turn that sucker on and make piles of sawdust, wood chips and other debris disappear.

I sensed that some folks were a little shocked with my dad's under-age assistant. But more often than not, I got kudos for the help I provided. "That's quite a helper you've got, Gus. How much are you paying this little guy? Can I just hire Sam for the day?" The positive reinforcement fueled a desire to take on more tasks and gain some of the nuances of good carpentry work. By the time I turned 14, I could make fairly good cuts with a circular saw, and deliver precise lengths from my dad's sliding compound saw.

When he called for a stair tread "36 inches strong," I knew to cut 1/16th of an inch past 36. A "weak" designation indicated an equally small subtraction from a given length.

I learned a lot about what can go wrong with a house: rotten exterior trim, roof leaks, doors that don't close properly, drafty windows, cracked floor tile. "It's kind of like being a doctor," my dad explained as we drove home in his truck late one afternoon. "You can't just treat the symptom. It's usually important to find out what caused the problem." When I asked for some examples, he didn't hesitate. "If the floor's too bouncy, you might need to beef up some undersized joists. Of if there's a water stain on the ceiling, you can't just patch in new drywall. You need to go up on the roof and find where the leak is."

Did my early work experience leave me feeling deprived of a "normal" childhood? That question didn't occur until I got into high school and encountered kids who grew up a lot differently. Sure, I knew plenty of kids who hung out in their rooms playing video games. But in the small town where we lived, I had other friends who helped out with the family business –at the local deli, dog kennel, gas station, or hardware store. Taking part in these adult enterprises never seemed like a negative, at least until I got into high school.

Even though my parents felt it was safe to leave me alone at home by the time I turned 12, I often went along with my dad to remodeling jobs –either out of habit, or because I enjoyed the compliments that came my way from different clients. Innate curiosity often played a role, too. The variety of jobs continued to fascinate me, along with all the different materials and construction techniques. I remember the first time I saw concrete sluicing into the foundation forms for a 2-car garage my dad built. I stood by as the mixer truck edged up to the excavation, and noted the sign language that workers used with each other as the truck's engine roared and the stone-filled slurry made its noisy way down the telescoping chute. It was amazing to see such competent control of messy material, and equally amazing to see the solid stem walls emerge a day later when we stripped off the forms.

During the summer of my 14th year, my dad started to pay me for helping him out. "Sam, your mom and I have talked it over," he explained one Saturday near the end of the school year. "I don't want you to feel like you have to work with me. You deserve to enjoy your summer vacation, just like the other kids your age." I nodded, and Dad continued. "The thing is, you're on your way to becoming a good carpenter."

"Thanks, Dad."

"I'm not gonna turn you down if you want to come along as my helper, but you deserve to get paid. How does $10 and hour sound?"

It sounded good to me at the time –quite a bit more money than I'd earned shoveling snow or raking leaves for neighbors, and more than most of my friends were making for various jobs. What my dad made clear was that if I agreed to come along on a job, I couldn't opt out at the last minute.

Chapter 2

My dad's work vehicle was always a late-model Ford F-150. I remember his trucks mostly by color –light blue when I was in grammar school, silver during my early teens, and a mean-looking black while I was in high school. When I turned 16 in May of 2007, my dad bought a used Toyota pickup for me to drive. It was a big deal. We didn't live in an affluent community, and there weren't many kids who got cars to go with their drivers' licenses. Of course, my father's motivation was mostly practical. Now he could send his helper to pick up building materials instead of taking on this time-consuming task himself.

The Tacoma was just a basic, no-frills vehicle, but I was thrilled to have it. Dad insisted on installing a heavy-duty rack for hauling the lumber we needed on many jobs. This bulky accessory definitely made the truck look clunkier than I liked, but I wasn't about to complain. I had my own ride.

The summer of my 16th year was memorable, and not just because I gained the independence and swagger that came with my own vehicle. Dad and I agreed that I would work four days a week, taking Monday or Friday off so that I always had a long weekend. Although I wanted to spend some summer days taking it easy and hanging out with friends, I was still caught up in the challenge of building up my repertoire of carpentry capabilities. Getting a raise to $15 and hour definitely sweetened the deal.

###

With her graduate degree in hand, my mom was primed to rejoin the job market. A week after the July 4th holiday, she learned that she'd be filling an opening in the English department at Kirkland Academy, a private school in Greenwich, CT. The school was about an hour's drive from our house, but it was a world away from the school experience I'd grown accustomed to. Kirkland Academy was just one of eight private schools catering to this exclusive community along the "Gold Coast," where investment bankers, top executives, and other millionaires made their homes. My mother's position on the faculty entitled me to free tuition. Both my parents thought that this $45,000-a-year value was too good to pass up.

But I'm not onboard with the plan at all.

"I don't want to go, Mom. What about all my friends here?" I asked. "I'll just be a stranger surrounded by rich kids." I was thinking about the classmates I'd known through grade school, and the new acquaintances I'd met during my freshman year at the regional high school. Then there were buddies I competed with on the track team, and the girls I'd begun to notice more and more.

Leaving that all behind for the uncharted territory of Kirkland seemed like an immense adolescent nightmare.

"I understand how you feel, Sam," my mom said, while exchanging a knowing look at Dad before turning back to me. "Look, we want you to give Kirkland a try. The quality of education you'll get is exceptional. That's not just coming from me. Anyone familiar with the school will tell you that."

"I didn't think there was anything wrong with our schools," I argued.

"It's not that, Sam," my mom responded. "I'm asking you to trust me on this. You'll get to do more and learn more at Kirkland. They keep class sizes small for a more intensive learning experience. You'll get to take field trips to museums in New York City, and attend special lectures by all kinds of experts and interesting people. It's more like college, actually. In fact, graduating from Kirkland will make a big difference when you apply to college."

It became clear to me that I wasn't going to win the argument about switching schools. I got a mix of responses when I shared the news with friends:

"Wow, I guess you'll be rubbing shoulders with the rich and famous, Sam."

"Don't sweat it, dude. You'll make a bunch of new buddies, and we can still hang out on weekends and vacations."

Then there was this request from Julie, who I ran into while gassing up the Tacoma. She belonged to a small group of girls who seemed to delight in driving guys to distraction. When I shared the news about Kirkland, she put in a simple request: "Sam, see if you can find me a nice-looking guy who just happens to super rich."

Yeah, sure.

I took a couple of trips to Kirkland that August. It was Mom's idea to take me along while she brought some supplies to her classroom, and had meetings with other faculty members. Some things about the school were familiar, like the hallways lined with lockers, the stenciled room numbers on classroom doors, and the smell of highly waxed floors. But some of the classrooms in the older section of the school –the original building dated back to 1902—looked more like the libraries or sitting rooms you'd find in a well-preserved Victorian-era home. Stepping into several of these smaller-sized classrooms with their wood-paneled walls, antique desks, and oak flooring made me feel like a character in an Indiana Jones movie.

Getting a preview of my new school was a good idea in theory, but it had my emotions bouncing between excitement, curiosity, and dread. My mom had plenty of answers to my questions about teachers, homework, and other academic issues, but I was more nervous about how I'd fit into this new adolescent ecosystem. *How difficult will it be to make new friends? Will I be able to make the track and cross-country teams? What are the girls like?*

There were practical reasons for me to drive the Tacoma to Kirkland, rather than riding in with my mom. I knew I'd be staying late for cross country practice or meets on most days, and Mom wanted to arrive earlier than me in the morning, in order to prep for classes. But I was also interested in the elevated status I'd enjoy for having my own vehicle as a sophomore –or so I thought. Big mistake. When I pulled into the designated student parking lot on my first day, the tarmac that had been empty during my summer visits was packed with vehicles vastly different from the Kias, Nissans, and Fords I was accustomed to seeing. Here we have a selection of shiny VWs and Audis, along with what looks to be a vintage MG and an equally pristine Fiat convertible. I also noticed that there wasn't a single yellow schoolbus in sight. Instead, a policeman directed a parade of BMWs and Mercedes into the school's main entrance. Yeah, my truck stood out in this crowd, but not in a good way.

The school's dress code didn't improve my comfort level. Instead of the jean-and-t-shirt wardrobe I'd grown used to, male students were required to wear pressed pants, button-down shirts, and "acceptable" shoes. I noticed that some upper-class members had jackets emblazoned with the school crest, a distinction I later learned was bestowed on "prefects" recognized for their leadership qualities.

The girls at Kirkland were beautiful, but they also seemed –at least in the beginning—to be totally unattainable. This initial impression probably had something to do with the more formal dress code, along with the perfect makeup, styled hair, and extreme confidence level that seemed to be the rule rather than the exception.

Chapter 3

I'd like to say that I adjusted well to my new school, but that wouldn't be entirely accurate. Mom was right about the academic stuff. I found myself enjoying the smaller classes and the novel ways that some of my teachers presented information. The social adjustment didn't go well. Most of the time, I felt out of place among the sons and daughters of parents who had family money or lucrative professions in New York City. Some of differences I encountered were obvious, like the late-model cars my classmates drove and the monogrammed shirts that many students wore. It was a new world of affluence I hadn't seen before. But that wasn't the tough part. The deeper cut was the ongoing commentary I got from certain classmates:

"Hey Sam, can you fit a mattress in your truck bed? That would make it a better chick magnet, right?"

"Guys, check out this crack in the gym floor. That's a job for our friend, Mr. Sawdust."

"I bet you didn't know why Sam has such big thumbs. It's because he keeps hitting them with his hammer."

I did my best to laugh off the jokes. But I had the same desire to fit in that every teenager does. The steady dose of ribbing affected me in different ways, depending on how things were going on a given day. Initially the carpentry jokes just caused surprise and confusion. I mean, up till now I'd just received praise and encouragement for the skills I'd learned. *Why are these kids making fun of me all of a sudden?* After a while, the teasing got old and made me angry. *Come on, can't you just treat me like any other classmate?*

I couldn't talk to my parents about these issues. Even my immature adolescent brain knew that sharing my hurt and embarrassment with them would upset what I'd come to understand as the family plan –a prime teaching position my mom had worked hard to attain, a quality education for me, and for my dad, access to an affluent community where contractors could double the rates they normally charged. It was clear that my parents were both happy with their new work situations, so I needed to get with the program.

That's what I did. It wasn't difficult to fit in on the school's track and cross-country teams. You know the deal: Sport is the great equalizer; social status has no bearing on how well you can compete. (There's more to say about running, but that has to wait till later.) Kirkland's challenging academic program enabled me to develop some friendships that just focused on studying and occasionally teaming up on class projects.

"Sam, you seem to be adjusting well to Kirkland," my mother observed as I began my second semester at school. Yeah, that was true in academic and sports areas, I thought to myself. But that comfort level disappeared in social situations. The cars, the clothes, the cash, the confidence; it was all bigger and better than anything I'd experienced before. But it's funny how things that seem so foreign at first can gradually become more normalized. I was an alien visitor the first time I got invited to a party at a classmate's house. But by the end of second year at Kirkland, I found myself getting used to the huge size of the homes I visited and "standard" features that initially blew me away; en-suite bathrooms, home theatres, exercise rooms full of expensive equipment, pools, guest houses, 3-car garages, and more. Sure, I still felt out of place. But a new thought started to percolate: Maybe this foreigner could gain citizenship somehow if he played his cards right. I started to get intrigued with the possibility.

One thing that changed was my relationship to carpentry. Look, there are plenty of reasons to develop a dislike for the work I'd been doing with my dad: the splinters you get while handling sheets of plywood, the filthy dust you inhale during demo work, the major blocks of time spent driving to distant jobsites, or the unforeseen problems that can complicate a project. I was always able to overlook these aggravations because of the praise that came my way growing up. But as my dad began to take on more work in Greenwich, I'd often find myself working at the home of a classmate. That's what happened more and more during the summers of my junior and senior years at Kirkland. Major remodeling jobs like kitchen makeovers meant multiple days under the casual observation of friends who could spend afternoons playing video games or hanging out around the backyard pool with their buddies.

Think about it: It's 9 am on Tuesday morning in July, and I'm in the driveway of the mega-mansion where Janet and Richard live. Richard (never "Dick" or "Ricky") is in my class at Kirkland; Janet (also a Kirkland student) is a year younger. I'm cutting sheets of drywall to size on sawhorses set up next to my truck, to help my dad turn part of their basement into an entertainment room. I've already sweat through my t-shirt, and when my classmates come outside on their way to the country club, I'm sporting a light coat of gypsum dust, stuck to the sweaty surfaces of my shirt, arms, and face.

This from Richard: "Hey Sam, you're covered in pixie dust! Why don't you take off that tool belt and come to the club with us?"

"Yeah, that would be nice," I say. But it wouldn't. I was pretty sure I'd feel massively out of place, even if I had the perfect outfits my classmates were wearing and a fancier vehicle to drive to the club. "Take a few extra laps in the pool for me," is all I can manage to end the conversation.

Scenes like this were repeated during the summers of my high school years. I'm sure my father was able to sense the embarrassment I felt at different times. But instead of asking me about it, he chose to do what he'd always done, praising my work, expressing his gratitude for having such a reliable helper, and paying a wage that I couldn't possibly have earned at other jobs. This positive reinforcement wasn't enough to deter me from the new plan I'd been formulating. I was determined to get through college, leave carpentry behind, and land a high-paying job that would put me in the white-collar world on Connecticut's Gold Coast.

Chapter 4

At Kirkland, I had plenty of girls who were friends; I'd dance with them at parties or just hang out with them at basketball games and other school events. The only serious girlfriend I had was an exchange student from Spain who was at school during my junior year. Christina came from a working-class family in Barcelona; I still haven't figured out how she got placed in an exclusive school like Kirkland. When she complimented me on the 10-year-old Tacoma I drove to school, I thought she was being sarcastic. But that wasn't the case.

"My brother, he also has this…. camioneta," she said, pointing at the truck. "He is working to make brick walls and chimneys."

"OK, he's a mason, I think that's what you mean," I said. "Here we call this a truck, Christina. My father is a carpenter, and I work with him sometimes." It took a while to explain the varied activities that remodeling work can involve, but Christina's interest in my life outside of school seemed genuine, and came as a welcome surprise. We had fun sharing the Spanish and English words for different carpentry tools.

Our school hadn't hosted an exchange student before, and Christina didn't have any easy time of it. I'm not sure why she was shunned by so many of her female classmates. It might have been the cruel competitiveness among teenage girls, or the same class-conscious snobbery I was encountering. As our familiarity grew during the time we spent in shared classes, study halls, and lunch periods, we puzzled over our outsider status. Although we didn't use that label to describe what we were experiencing, it was a frequent theme in our conversations. We marveled at the different manifestations of wealth that most of our classmates took for granted.

I thought Christina was beautiful. She had dark hair, a tawny complexion, and the deepest, darkest eyes I'd ever seen. My parents urged me to invite her to dinner as our relationship deepened, but I was hesitant –mostly because of how our modest house contrasted with the residence of Christina's host family and all the other Gold Coast mansions. But I needn't have worried. "This is more like my home," she said, after looking around our place before her first dinner at our house. My parents liked Christina right away, recognizing –I think—that at least some of the foreignness she felt wasn't about language but about status and the trappings of wealth.

By Thanksgiving of my junior year, we had pretty much become girlfriend and boyfriend, spending bunches of time together at school and on weekends. Christina even came to a couple of my cross-country meets, joining a few parents who bundled up against the autumn chill to see a handful of runners scramble over the uneven terrain that was our home course.

As we age and go through life, the word "love" becomes heavy with the freight of missteps, misunderstandings, anxieties and insecurities. The love that developed between Christina and me didn't have such baggage. We were both cautious, guarded people. Our progression from friendship to physical expressions of affection proceeded in small increments, aided by the realization that we had similar levels of sexual inexperience to overcome. What happened was markedly different from the brief episodes of alcohol-fueled groping that I had done prior to meeting Christina. I'll admit that a good measure of my awkwardness had its origins in a serious and embarrassing discussion initiated by my mother prior to my freshman year. The rigorous orientation program she was required to take as a new Kirkland employee included a major workshop on sexual harassment. So she wasn't about to make assumptions about her son's judgment and behavior in matters of sex. I got the full-blown dissertation on safe sex, consent, and the life-changing consequences of bad behavior.

With a strange mix of curiosity, desire, and fumbling around, Christina and I explored different ways to have sex without having intercourse. I didn't feel deprived; in fact I admired Christina for setting a boundary based on her Catholic upbringing. As it turned out, my mother's advice came in handy, helping both of us learn from each other, and laugh our way through a few awkward moments.

My relationship with Christina was a turning point in other ways, too. I remember feeling happy and secure for the first time since I entering the school. But the bliss didn't last. A week after Thanksgiving, Christina got word that her father had suffered a heart attack. She flew back to Spain to be with her family. Although her father survived and was convalescing, his incapacity seemed to demand the involvement of all family members, at least as far as I could tell. When we spoke on the phone, it was clear that Christina was overwhelmed by family responsibilities. I missed her, and it was devastating to hear that she wasn't going to be coming back to finish out her exchange year.

Chapter 5

Part of Kirkland's mission to "enrich the mind, body, and spirit" of every student called for universal participation in sports. This mandate applied regardless of ability level; even students with disabilities were encouraged and accommodated. My reasons for choosing to be a runner on the track and cross-country teams only became clear to me much later in life.

What I now understand is that choosing a solitary sport effectively spared me some of the subtle but steady reminders that I was different from the guys who joined the football, basketball and baseball teams. Track and cross country were, after all, the sports chosen by outsiders and wierdos. With my lanky frame, social awkwardness, and ability to pace myself through long days of manual labor, I had the raw ingredients to make a decent long-distance runner. The cross-country season was in the fall, while track took place in the spring. Neither sport was popular at our school, so it wasn't a stellar achievement for me to carve out a top spot on both teams. In my junior and senior years, I qualified for the state championships that took place near the end of each season.

Running wasn't the sport you chose to attract girls. No, that would be football and basketball, where every game draws a crowd and includes a squad of cheerleaders. But I don't regret all the miles I logged, or the track meets where coaches and team members where the only spectators. What I came to appreciate was the simplicity and economy of running. It just takes a pair of sneakers, and some inexpensive clothes selected to match the weather conditions. Whether it's a solitary jog or a race with others, you're really competing against yourself, seeing how hard and how long you can push your body. As I grappled with the raging hormones and emotional upheavals of adolescent life, running became valuable as a way to clear my head, and enjoy a brief endorphin high that could sometimes brighten my outlook.

There were a couple of events that left major marks during my last two years of high school. The first of these you already know about –my relationship with Christina, disrupted suddenly by her early return to Spain following her father's heart attack. The second event occurred during the summer following my senior year, while I was working on a small pool house in New Canaan. It wasn't the first job we did for the Evans family, which included Grant and Julia, who also attended Kirkland. A year earlier, my dad and I spent several weeks finishing their basement. We created a media room tricked out with reclaimed barn siding on the walls, a nice mini-bar, and built-in cabinetry that flanked a large TV screen. The job really came out well, and the breadth of the work had real skill-building value for me. My dad and I handled everything from framing and flooring to insulation, rough wiring, and trim carpentry. But what I remember most about the project was a succession of sunny summer days spent in a dark basement while the Evans family hung out around their pool or went sailing with friends.

Plans for the pool house were drawn up by a local architect – definitely overkill for a 16ft. x 20ft. outbuilding. After looking over the design sometime in May, Dad had to break the news to the Evans family that the project probably wouldn't be finished until mid- to late summer. He was good at explaining the complexities of construction to customers. I can remember this conversation, as well as many others, from that summer.

"We'll need to get a machine into the backyard to excavate for the slab," he began. "We'll also need to dig trenches for plumbing and electric lines. After the slab has been poured, we can begin to frame up the structure. It will be mid-July by the time we get the building weathered in and begin with interior finish work."

This wasn't the news that Carl and Bridget Evans wanted to hear, and their initial response was to pressure my dad to put other projects on hold and get the pool house started immediately. But this request was nullified a few days later when Mr. Evans let us know about some new plans for the summer. "We don't want a rush job on the pool house," he said. "We want you to have the time to do it right. So, we're taking the boat up to Maine in June. We've got a friend with a big place on Mount Desert Island, and he's promised us plenty of sailing, golf, and hiking."

I didn't give the project much thought after we heard from Mr. Evans. To me, it was just another job to fill up the summer, and at least I wouldn't be spending it in a basement. Besides, I was doing my best to study for final exams, and have some fun with friends. Just a few weeks before, I'd received a letter of acceptance from UConn, and I was excited about starting my freshman year in the fall.

Dad had lined up a bunch of projects to begin after school closed for the summer, anticipating the extra capacity that I'd provide, along with occasional help from Mr. Harper, who appreciated the opportunity to augment his teaching salary. We had a series of deck jobs –a mix of new construction and renovation work. Outdoor carpentry work is definitely preferable to the indoor variety. You can spend your days in shorts and a t-shirt, get a nice tan, and have plenty of daylight left over when work stops at 5:00 or so. Indoor remodeling work is much more stressful because you're always worried about dropping a tool on the floor, knocking over a lamp, or doing other accidental damage.

Near the end of June, we were just about ready to tackle the pool house project. That's when I got a call from Grant Evans. He asked me how my summer was going, but then interrupted me before I could answer.

"You'll never guess what happened yesterday, Sam. My Mom broke her ankle falling off her exercise bike."

"Wow, that's bad," I offered. "How can something like that happen?"

Grant seemed just as astonished as I was. "That's the thing. My dad bought her a new stationary bike for her birthday a few weeks ago. I helped him assemble it but it looks like we didn't get the rear stand attached the right way. She fell off right in the middle of a workout, and the bike fell on top of her."

"Damn, I'm sorry to hear that," I said. "How bad is it?"

"You wouldn't think that you could get hurt just falling off a bike," Grant reasoned. "But I guess her foot got trapped in the bike frame when she fell, and the weight of the bike caused a pretty bad break. She's got a cast from her foot all the way up to mid-thigh."

"So, what does this mean for your summer plans?" I asked, thinking about the pool house project.

"The 'rents had a big argument last night," said Grant. "It looks like Mom is going to stay here, since she can't do much. The rest of us are heading up next week. The cast can't come off till the middle of August. "

"OK, good to know, Grant. Look, maybe that will work out for the best. We'll be building the pool house, so we'll be around if your mom needs help. Give her my best."

At dinner that night I learned that my dad had a similar conversation with Carl Evans. "It shouldn't affect our plans for the project," he said. "If anything, it will be an incentive to keep the jobsite neat and well organized, and that's not a bad thing."

A few days later, Dad and I went over to stake out the excavation for the slab, and figure out the best place to offload all the framing lumber. Mrs. Evans waved us over from her front door, and seemed to be in good spirits. "Gus and Sam! I'm glad you're getting started," she said. "I hope you'll excuse my attire. This monster cast is limiting my wardrobe choices." Yes, the cast was substantial, but it was also unusual to see Grant's mom in giant-size gym shorts and a loosely fitting t-shirt. This was a lady I was accustomed to seeing in fashionable, well-fitting outfits. The oversize clothes, combined with a short, pixie-ish haircut, made her seem younger and –to my overactive adolescent radar— attractive in a way that made me feel strange.

"It's good to see you up and about," my dad replied. "Sorry you're missing out on the Maine vacation."

"It's for the best. I didn't want to be stuck up there in the guest house, feeling sorry for myself while everyone was out waterskiing or sailing or doing other fun stuff. "

"Well, I'm glad we're going to get started on your project," my dad offered. "The excavator is coming tomorrow, and we'll pour the slab at the end of the week."

Looking past Mrs. Evans into the kitchen, I saw a large supply of groceries spread across the countertop. "How are you getting food and supplies and stuff?" I asked.

"I'm paying my cleaning lady to do the shopping for me every few days," she replied. "And I'm managing to hobble around the house with this," she said, gesturing with the aluminum crutch she'd been leaning on. "I can't handle the stairs, so we set up a bed in the living room."

The job started well. By the end of the first week, we had backfilled around the slab and begun to frame the structure's exterior walls. Then the forecast of a severe storm with high winds had my dad and I scrambling to tie down all the building materials, and install temporary bracing on the walls we'd erected so that the wind wouldn't blow them down.

Everyone battened down for a bad storm, and during its short duration –just one afternoon and the better part of the next day— there was a tremendous amount of damage. We lost power just before I went to bed, but it was back on when I woke up. The coastal communities where my dad did most of his work really got hammered. After the storm passed through, Dad called Mrs. Evans to find out how the partially built pool house had held up. "No problems I can see," she reported. "The backyard is covered with loads of debris, but it looks like the walls you built are fine."

The good news didn't last. Before the morning was out, Dad got half a dozen calls from customers whose homes had been damaged. Falling trees had crashed through the roofs of two houses and destroyed a couple of decks. Other clients needed broken windows or skylights replaced.

"What a nightmare," my mom said. "You can't possibly take on all these emergency repairs."

I could tell that my father was worried. "You're right, Jean. Even with Sam and Rick working full time, we can't possibly handle all these repairs. Sam, we'll need to prioritize these jobs and get some kind of schedule together."

"Look Dad," I offered, "I can work solo on the pool house while you and Mr. Harper tackle all this repair work. I might need a little help with the roof framing, but I can let you know. I mean, there's no rush to get the pool house finished, right? Mrs. Evans can't use it, and the rest of the family is in Maine for the summer."

After thinking over my offer for a while, Dad agreed to keep me on the pool house project, while he and Mr. Harper coped with the storm damage repairs. I was glad for the opportunity to be working on my own. When I arrived at the Evans house, there were broken twigs and small tree branches everywhere. I knocked on the front door to let Mrs. Evans know I was there. She came to the door in what looked to be the same t-shirt and oversize shorts she'd worn before.

"Hi Sam, I'm glad you're here," she said. "We got lucky, I guess. No loss of power, and no fallen trees."

"Yeah, my dad got a bunch of calls from folks who had major damage. Caved-in roofs, broken windows, damaged decks. If it's OK with you, I'm going to keep working on the pool house while Dad and Mr. Harper help out folks who need emergency repairs."

"Sure, that's fine, Sam."

Good to get that cleared up. "I can't see any structural damage to the walls we built, or anywhere else," I said. "Just a lot of tree debris."

She raised her arm to scratch her head, revealing part of a bare breast inside the oversized sleeve of her t-shirt, along with an unshaven armpit. I couldn't look away, even though my brain was telling me to. Nor could I understand how the raw version of Mrs. E (so different from the well-appointed lady I was accustomed to seeing) could have such a different effect on me. What is happening here?

"Sam?"

I wasn't paying attention. "Sorry, Mrs. E.," I said, with as much composure as I could muster. "What were you saying?"

Why is she smiling? "Would you mind taking a few minutes before you leave today to get the twigs and leaves out of the pool? I'm afraid they might clog up the filter."

"Sure, Mrs. E. I'll get it done before I leave."

I don't normally resort to verbally berating myself. But once she closed the door and I headed back to my truck to unload some tools, I had to make an exception. *Why can't you shut down your lizard brain? This is Grant's mother, remember! Think about carpentry, you moron.* But part of the troubling dialog going on in my head had an explanation for my inappropriate attraction. The sexual exploration I'd been enjoying with Christina had ended suddenly over six months ago. I missed it, just as anyone would. I just didn't expect the mother of a classmate to displace Christina in my fantasies.

The weather that followed the storm was bright and clear. I framed the remaining exterior walls flat on the slab, after double-checking the rough openings for windows and doors as indicated in the plans. Dad stopped by at the end of day to help tilt up the walls and brace them plumb. Of course, I knew he also wanted to check my work because we'd normally be doing a project like this together. We went over the details for getting the ridge board installed and cutting the rafters.

"It looks like you're doing a good job, Sam," he said.

"Yeah, but it's slow going with just me here," I commented.

"Do you want me or Rick to .."

"No, I'm good on my own," I jumped in. "I mean, it's not like Mrs. Evans is complaining or anything."

"So, you're getting on OK with her?" he asked.

"I think it's going well," I answered. "She comes out and waves from the deck. I think it's too difficult for her to come down the deck stairs to get a closer look."

Reassuring my dad that the project was going well was important to me, but not in any professional sense. To put it bluntly, I didn't want anyone interrupting the relationship that was developing between Mrs. E and me. Every time I gave my dad a progress report on the pool house, I was conscious of details I was leaving out. Like how Mrs. E. would sunbathe on the deck, replacing her oversize t-shirt and shorts with a tiny yellow bikini that distracted the hell out of me. Or how I'd been taking a quick dip in the pool before heading home at the end of the day. The swim was Mrs. E's idea, and after working in 90° heat for 8 hours, the pool was a refreshing way to remove the slimy layer of sweat and sawdust that coated my face, arms, and legs. She'd often lean over the deck railing as I was toweling off, pretending to re-tie the strings on the bikini top that she'd left undone for sunbathing. I tried not to stare as we discussed different topics –everything from TV shows and current events to stuff about school and relationships.

It wasn't just the flirtation that had me captivated. Mrs. E seemed fascinated with the process of transforming a pile of lumber into a building. OK, I know she didn't have a lot of other activities to focus on, but I wasn't used to clients showing interest or appreciation for the work done by a carpenter. It made me feel good to explain some of the tricks I'd learned from my dad, like going through a pile of framing lumber to select the straightest, clearest 2x4s for the king and jack studs used to frame door and window openings.

Chapter 6

Carpentry work isn't a great way to stay in shape. Sure, it can provide upper body strength with all the lifting and tool use that goes on. But it sucks at developing the aerobic fitness that I needed as a distance runner. During the summer, I'd keep in shape for track by jogging on a couple of weekday afternoons, and by taking longer runs on Sundays. My dad was pretty good about letting me quit early on Tuesdays and Thursdays, so I could head home and then head out to log some miles.

Once the pool house project got underway, I started to do my weekday runs right from the Evans house. After packing up my tools and cleaning up the jobsite around 5:00, I'd change into my running gear and jog over to the school track, where I could actually time myself and do some of the interval training I'd learned from Mr. Harper. When I was done, I'd make the short jog back to the Evans house, cool off in the pool for a few minutes, then change into dry clothes and head home.

A couple of weeks into this new running routine, I found Mrs. Evans at the bottom of the deck stairs when I got back from my Thursday run. I had just peeled off my sweat-soaked shirt, thrown it in the truck, and grabbed the towel I kept behind the passenger seat. I saw her as soon as I headed down to the pool, sitting awkwardly on the concrete pad at base of the stairs.

"What happened? Are you OK?" I asked.

"I feel so stupid," she replied. "I dropped my phone off the deck after you left, then fell down the stairs when I was trying to get it." She started to laugh, then started to cry. I wasn't sure how to respond to the juxtaposed emotions, and I think she recognized my confusion. "I'm sorry, Sam," she said a moment later. "I'm just so sick of hobbling around with this fucking cast."

I noticed some blood on her ankle, just below the bottom of her cast. "Are you sure you're not hurt? It looks like you're bleeding there." As I pointed to her ankle, I realized that she was just wearing white cotton underwear and a t-shirt with no bra. All kinds of awkward thoughts began to fly through my head.

"Oh, yeah, I guess I did get a scrape. My leg's fine, though. Can you help me back up the stairs?"

"Sure, Mrs. E. But I'm kinda sweaty and gross from my run."

"That's OK, Sam. Let's just make the best of it."

I bent down behind her, reached under her arms, and lifted her up, feeling her breasts flop onto my forearms. Then we hobbled up the steps, her arm around my waist, and my arm around hers. It was more than I bargained for: sweaty, sticky skin against skin, with some musky odor thrown in for good measure. The sensory overload I experienced included the sound of our breathing as our bodies moved together. I had the distinct feeling that something happened in the short space of those seven steps. When we reached the deck, the time came for Mrs. E to let go of me and grab the crutches that were leaning against the deck railing. But instead, she turned and hugged me with both arms, pushing her breasts against my chest and leaning her head against my bare shoulder. A moment later she looked into my eyes and kissed me.

It wasn't a motherly kiss, and I didn't want it to be. Even though I knew it was wrong. Even though I knew that the feelings I'd been having for several weeks needed to be directed at someone my own age.

"Take me inside, Sam," she said. When we stepped into the living room, I hesitated, not knowing where she wanted to go. "Come with me," she said, hobbling towards the den, where her bed was set up.

We didn't exchange many words after that. When I eased Mrs. E down onto her bed, she looked up at me, and removed her t-shirt before lying down under the bedsheet. I took off my sneakers and shorts, then slipped in beside her, wondering how this could be happening, but not wanting anything to be different. She surely sensed this conflict, turning toward me, putting her arms around me, and whispering softly. "Sam, Sam, Sam, you're so sweet. I want to kiss some more while you feel my breasts." This I could do. After what seemed like just a few moments, she pushed my hand down between her legs and grabbed my erection. In a short span of time the senses of smell, touch and feel overwhelmed any moral quandaries I had been struggling with. But I hesitated for a moment when she said "I want you inside me," aware of my own inexperience and the difficulties posed by the cast on her leg. When I started to move over her, she countered: "No, Sam, it won't work that way. You'll have to come in from behind me. "

And so it went. It wasn't the way I'd envisioned losing my virginity, but it was intensely erotic just the same. We climaxed a few moments apart, propelled by the little gasps she made while turning her head to kiss me, and by my fingers caressing the place that Christina had revealed to me in what now seemed a distant era of my life.

There wasn't much of an awkward silence when we broke our spooning embrace, mainly because I noticed spots of blood on the bedsheet that had temporarily entwined us before being kicked out of the way. "Don't worry, Sam; I'm sure it's from the cut on my ankle," Mrs. E explained. Yeah, I'd forgotten about the abrasion from her fall down the stairs.

"Are you sure you can even reach that cut to put a band-aid on?" I asked. "You can't bend your leg because of the cast. Tell me where I can find some ointment and band-aids."

She tried stretching down the length of the cast, then laughed. "You're right, I could use some help here. And you've already helped in a pretty special way, Sam. I've been obsessing about sex lately. It's not like I have lots of activities to look forward to every day. And the pain meds I've been taking have the side effect of making me horny. I've heard that's not uncommon."

"Mrs. E, I.."

"I know it's wrong," she interrupted. "I'm married and I'm old,
…

"You're beautiful and sexy, Mrs. E."

"Oh God, what a sweet thing for you to say. Look, I've had plenty of time lately to think about where I am in this life. I've got a husband who would rather spend time on the golf course or on his boat than with me. I'd forgotten what it's like to be desired and to desire someone. When you get something back that you thought was lost, …" Instead of finishing the sentence, she just smiled at me.

I didn't know how to reply. "Why don't I get that stuff for your leg?" I offered, quickly putting on my shorts. When I got back from the bathroom with a box of band-aids and some antiseptic ointment, Mrs. E was sitting up in bed with her t-shirt back on. She pulled the sheet off her legs so I could get to her ankle, revealing the white cotton panties that had been stretched out of the way when I…. Oh my God…. I sat down on the edge of the bed and lifted her cast onto my lap. I tried to focus on just bandaging the injury, but the closeness of our bodies and smell of our sex was overwhelming. When I finished pressing the band-aid in place, Mrs. E pulled me back up against her.

Chapter 7

Driving home a while later, I tried in vain to gain some sort of perspective on what had just happened. Yes, I was dealing with erotic overload –a kaleidoscope of images, smells, and sounds that made it difficult to concentrate on driving. But I was also being pulled in the opposite direction, stressing about what my parents would think if they knew about this tryst. The territory between these emotional extremes got plenty of play too, as I wondered how and why things change between married couples.

None of this emotional turmoil had diminished when I drove to the Evans house the next day. For once, I was grateful for the painstaking carpentry work that lay ahead. Earlier in the week, I had finished installing all of the pool house's windows and doors. What came next –trimming around these openings—involved making some tricky cuts and pocket joinery in expensive synthetic trim stock. The work was as effective a distraction as I could have hoped for. I made good progress before breaking for lunch around 12:30. By that time, most of my body was covered with fine white dust and shavings, a predictable condition when working with plastic lumber. Sitting down to eat on a bench near the new building, I saw Mrs. E leaning over the deck railing.

"Sam, the pool house looks great," she said. "but you look like you've been in a snowstorm."

"Yeah, this plastic trim material always does that," I said, brushing a small dust cloud from the front of my shirt.

"Can you come up when you're done at the end of the day? I'd like to talk."

"Sure," I replied. The rest of the afternoon seemed to drag on forever. Between wondering about what would happen in a few hours, and reliving the previous day's activities, it's a wonder I didn't cut off my hand on the chopsaw. When 4:30 finally arrived, I started to clean up the day's mess –collecting all the offcuts and other lumber scraps, moving the tools inside the pool house, coiling up the extension cords, and (last but not least) doing my best to vacuum the white dust from my body.

When I shut off the vac, I heard Mrs. E up on the deck. "I'm up here," she beckoned. I walked up the same stairs that had worked magic the day before, and sat down next to her in a deck chair.

"Sam, I know what happened yesterday was wrong."

OK, I had a strong feeling that's where we'd begin, and I'd fabricated a smartass reply about us both being consenting adults, having just turned 18 at the beginning of the summer. But that's not what came out. "That was my first time, uh, you know…"

"Are you trying to tell me I took your virginity?" she asked. I nodded. "Oh brother, that makes me feel even worse," she said.

"No, please don't think that," I replied. "I really wanted to have sex with you. I mean, I've wanted to for a while," I confessed. "I know you're married, and older, and all that. It's just that, I can't stop thinking about …."

I never finished that sentence. Mrs. E reached over from her chair, took my hand, and pulled us together. Then she said those words again: "Let's go inside."

Chapter 8

It would have been helpful to talk to someone about my
relationship with Bridget Evans. No, let's be more specific: I
needed professional help from a good therapist. Someone who
could help me sort through the confusion of feelings that bounced
around in my head every day during the month-long duration of
our affair. The way that every day began with large measures of
guilt and fear playing off each other, only to be overcome by shear
horniness as I imagined and anticipated the lovemaking that would
–I hoped—take place when I finished work at the end of the day.
Well, let's be more accurate: There were a few lunchtime sessions,
too. The sex we had together was erotic in ways I couldn't have
imagined –instructive as well as exciting, with moments of humor
and tenderness interwoven with the passion.

Perhaps the relationship's intensity had something to do with
the fact that we both knew when this affair would come to an end.
The rest of the Evans family would be returning in mid-August,
about the same time the pool house project would be finished. And
I'd be heading off to UConn's freshman orientation the first week
of September.

My dad took a couple of days off from his storm recovery work
to help me with the finishing touches at the Evans house: an
undermount sink and mini-fridge in the bar area, crown molding
throughout the interior, and a decorative cupola for the roof. "You

did a nice job here, Sam," my dad said. "I'm proud of the way you handled this project on your own." Yeah, if he only knew. Just a day after we packed up our tools, the rest of the Evans family returned from Maine. Grant Evans called a week later and invited me over to hang out at the pool and enjoy the completed pool house. "C'mon, dude, you did such a great job on this project," he urged, "You deserve to kick back and enjoy the fruits of your labor."

I couldn't bring myself to accept the invitation. I wasn't sure what emotions would wash over me if I saw Mrs. E in her "normal" role again, but it seemed too risky a prospect. The only therapy I could come up with was to up my running regimen, taking time out of every day to jog some well-known routes through and around our little town. Dad gave me the last two weeks of the summer off, so it was easy to fit in the extra exercise. My parents figured that I was just interested in getting extra fit to compete in college. But the true reason for the extra running was to be alone with my thoughts while extra endorphins were pumping through my system. I knew the cycle my body went through on a typical run. For the first mile or so, the message getting through to my brain went something like this: *Hey, this is hard! Slow it down*! But with a steady, even pace established and some endorphins in my circulation, I could cruise for a good 20 or 30 minutes without being aware of pain or strain. That's when I could indulge in an inner dialog that seemed to help me, even though it produced more questions than answers. *What was the difference between the love I felt for Christina and the love I felt for Mrs. E? Can two people love each other, even when they know it can't last? Will I be able to find the same level of passion and companionship with someone my own age?*

My two weeks at home dragged on, and it was a relief to arrive on campus and join the melee of students who, like me, were intimidated and energized by their first year in college. I have many memories of that first semester. Most of them have to do with how overwhelmed I felt –by the size and diversity of the student body, the huge campus, the selection of majors and courses available, and even the variety of food at different campus cafeterias.

After a summer of steady physical labor, it seemed luxurious to spend hours sitting in a classroom. *Yeah, I can do this.* The only other activities in my schedule were training with the track team, and putting in 8 hours of work per week for the head of the campus theatre –the work/study arrangement that was part of my financial aid package. Listing carpentry as a skill on my college application got the attention of Mr. Winters, head of the theatre department. He needed help cleaning up and organizing all the lumber and other building materials used to build props and sets, so there I was. I don't think I ever put in the full 8 hours a week; it was usually more like 6. But it wasn't difficult to improve on the mess that I found in the storage and workshop areas backstage, so I never got any complaints about my job.

PART 2

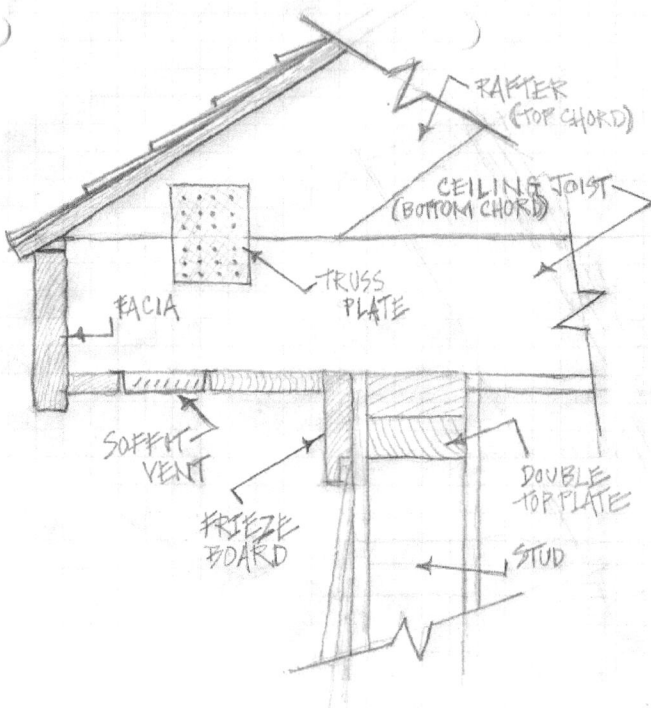

Framing

the act, process, or manner of constructing anything. The act of providing with a frame or a system of frames; framework. (CONSTRUCTION) the assembly of components –lumber, fasteners, hardware—that form the structure of a building.

Chapter 9

Don't worry; there's no plan to bore you with a detailed account of my college years. There's more important territory to cover, and my time at school progressed as anyone might have expected, with the requisite mix of studying, partying, drinking, mild drug use, and friendships that owed their development to academics, athletics, sexual attraction, or simple happenstance. I declared a major in marketing at the end of my freshman year, and worked with my academic advisor to chart a course program. Where did the interest in marketing come from? Good question. I think my mother's belief in the power of language gave me a strong interest in many aspects of marketing. But probably the most motivating factor in my career choice had to do with my uncle, who worked for an advertising agency in the city, and always regaled us with stories of meeting interesting people and coming up with offbeat but effective slogans or strategies for various marketing campaigns. It sounded like lots of fun, it paid well, and it had nothing to do with carpentry. I also liked what my academic advisor said about this professional path: "Sam, our entire economy is driven by marketing. It's a career with plenty of job security."

Until the end of my junior year in college, I still spent summers working with my dad, mainly because I could earn more with my carpentry skills than by other means. The recession that hit in 2008 caused a temporary slowdown for my dad's remodeling business. But his years of cultivating clients in the uber-affluent communities of Greenwich, Darien, New Canaan and Westport paid off during the recovery period. My parents weren't financially adept, but they had managed to accumulate enough savings to partially pay for my college education. I was able to make up the difference with a good a financial aid package that included a student loan and my part-time job on campus.

The affair with Mrs. E left an emotional mark that stayed with me a long time. I relived our time together –not just the sex, but the openness we had with each other in discussing all kinds of topics. Her marriage, my future, the growing digital universe that was enveloping us, and more. I never thought that this relationship would be the benchmark I used measure the relationships I was developing with the girls I met in college. But it was. And it left me with little patience for the pettiness, posturing, and immaturity I often encountered.

In the summer that followed my junior year at UConn, my academic advisor landed me an internship at an advertising agency in Stamford. Brad Parks, the agency owner, had a couple of children I knew from high school. The internship went well, and Brad told me to come back after I graduated. So that's where I landed.

Both my parents were still working, although when I graduated in 2010, my dad was being more selective about the jobs he took, willing to make less money in exchange for a little less stress. I initially stayed with them and commuted in to Stamford, but within a couple of months I had found a small apartment on the third floor of an older building just a few miles from work.

Because of my carpentry experience, Brad had me work with a couple of building supply businesses who were clients. Of course, I started out at the bottom of the ladder, as an assistant account executive. But I was fine with that. What seemed important at the time was that I'd made my escape from carpentry work, and I was living on my own. But things got even better at the end of that first summer after graduation. That's when I gained some extra responsibilities at the agency that enhanced my job satisfaction, and –so I thought at the time—provided an extra measure of job security. I was put in charge of the sports sponsorship program that helped to elevate the company's visibility and good will in the community. This mostly involved the local softball league that operated in the summer and a winter basketball league. We provided uniforms and equipment emblazoned with the agency logo, and it was my job to publicize our sponsorship in as many ways as possible. It wasn't a promotion, but it seemed like a great vote of confidence. I was getting paid to interact with the coaches and players of local sports teams, take publicity photos at games, and feed scores and story ideas to local newspapers. It was fun, just as my uncle promised it would be.

I was fulfilling my fantasy of joining the well-to-do, white-collar world I had admired from a distance for most of my life. There were frequent trips into New York to attend parties, meet up at bars, and attend concerts or other special events. I wasn't saving much money, but I was putting on a good show for the affluent young professionals I so wanted to emulate. Spinning around in this whirlwind of activities blinded me to some danger signs that now seem obvious. The hours and energy I put into the sports sponsorship program enabled me to ignore the fact that I wasn't getting more responsibilities in managing client accounts. The truth was that there was little in my past that could have prepared me for the subtle maneuverings necessary to succeed in the corporate arena. The idea of forming strategic alliances with key people and always looking for ways to better my situation never occurred to me. I just thought that if I did a good job the right things would happen.

There were danger signs in my life outside of work too, but I was too caught up in my fast-paced lifestyle to notice. Jogging had long been a mainstay of physical and mental health for me, but I traded that habit in for a health club membership. Fine, in theory. The trouble was, my visits to Total Fitness dwindled down to once a week or so. A new favorite after-work activity developed: having drinks at any of several popular watering holes in close proximity to the office. It was a tradeoff I slipped into: gaining weight and getting out of shape in order to hang out with fellow young professionals. I'd occasionally run into a high school classmate – someone who worked locally or commuted to the city. I even saw Grant Evans a couple of times, at a bar close to the Greenwich train station. Yeah, Mr. and Mrs. E were still together. "Same old, same old," as Grant put it.

I still didn't have anything close to a steady girlfriend. Looking back, I can see how ridiculous my expectation was –to find a young, single, college-educated professional pursuing a similar level of inebriation, and just waiting for me to introduce myself. Most of the women I met in my new haunts had emotional baggage that ruled out any interaction beyond a one-night stand. My new pastime enabled me to develop the useless skill of guessing the affliction: divorced, separated, or still married but on the prowl for an ego-boosting adventure.

I should have had the wisdom and willpower to break out of this cycle. But I was convinced that a few drinks after work, or at a game, didn't put me close to the alcoholic cliché I had learned about growing up. Sure, I might have failed the breathalyzer test if I got stopped on the drive home. But that never happened, and (here's the real myth) because I didn't drink during the day (except for a few beers at Saturday games), I didn't have a problem. Or so I thought.

Chapter 10

In the cycle of addiction, I was heading towards my bottom –a level of degradation that has life-changing consequences. Its arrival began unexpectedly on a Friday in the middle of June, close to two years after I started at the agency. Things were going well, or so I thought. On the drive in to work, I picked up several boxes of new t-shirts I was planning to hand out to softball teams later in the week. The trunk of my car was full of new bats and balls, all part of the sponsorship package the company provided. I remember how clear and bright the day was as I pulled into the parking lot at the office. When I got to my desk, I found a note from Brad, the owner of the agency. It said: "Come see me when you get in." No sweat. Brad and I touched base on a regular basis –sometimes about the sponsorship program, other times about a client or ad campaign that involved me.

Asking me to close the door when I entered his office was the first trouble sign. I nodded a greeting as I sat down in my usual spot, in one of several comfortable chairs that faced his desk. I noticed a serious expression on Brad's face as he closed his laptop. "We're going to be restructuring the company, Sam," he said. "Social media just keeps getting bigger and bigger, and the agency needs to reallocate resources in that direction."

"Sure, I get that," I said.

"We're going to be discontinuing the team sponsorship program, Sam." That wasn't good news, but Brad wasn't done yet. "I've hired two new account executives from New York who are social media superstars. We're also getting a new IT guy to stay on top of all the challenges we'll be facing with online content management systems."

"That all makes sense, Brad," I said, "but it will be tough to break the news about sponsorship to all the teams I've been working with."

"You're right, Sam. I'll take care of that. The bad news is that we need to let you go. I'm sorry about this. You've been a valuable member of the team here, and you're well liked. But you're not the right fit for the new initiatives we're going to be pursuing."

"Wow" That's all I could say for a few seconds. Was this really happening? I struggled to stay calm, fighting the urge to cry. "I've never been fired before," I managed to blurt out.

"Look, Sam, this is just the start of your career. I'll write you a great recommendation, and you'll land a new job in no time." Yeah, well that's easy for you to say, I thought.

"When will this…, I mean, how soon..?"

Brad had his answers ready. "Today's your last day, Sam. But you'll get two week's severance pay. Kathy has a check waiting for you. The rest of the crew here already know about these changes. So, take your time gathering up your stuff, and saying goodbye. Like I said, I'm sorry this didn't work out. But you've made some good contacts and learned a lot in the short time you've been here. I know you'll do well."

I didn't really feel like hanging around after that. It was humiliating to know that the rest of the company already had this news. As I walked through the office, I'm sure the look on my face said it all. The sympathetic words I got from a few of my co-workers did little to allay the shock and hurt. When I got to my car and saw the softball team t-shirts in the back seat, it was another body blow. *Shit. Shit. Shit.*

Fired at 9:30 on a Friday morning. I wasn't sure what to do, or where to go. The next time I looked at my watch it was a few minutes after 3:00 in the afternoon. At that time, I was sitting alone in the bleachers at one of the many ball fields on the outskirts of town. I had a half-empty case of beer on my right and a growing pile of empties in a paper bag on my left. Crumpled bags of chips and peanuts littered the ground beneath the stands. I realized that I should have called my parents with the news when I left the office. Now it was too late because of my shitfaced state.

When I got down to my last two beers, something compelled me to retrieve some bats and softballs from the trunk of my car and put them to use on the ball field. Momentarily, my intoxication provided some distracting entertainment, as I tossed balls in the air and tried to hit them squarely with the bat. It was an exercise I normally did adeptly at team practices. But now I got to comment on my spastic performance.

"A swing and a miss. Did you see that folks? He nearly fell over when he wiffed on that pitch! Foul ball! That's two strikes; it's not lookin' good for this guy."

The next thing I remember is riding in the back of a police car, telling the officers up front to pull over so I could puke on the side of the road. Somehow, I managed to barf up a massive quantity of frothy liquid without significantly messing up my clothes. When we got to the police station, they told me (for the second time, apparently) that I'd been arrested for drunk and disorderly conduct, and for harming public property. I found out later that at some point in my drunken batting session, I'd taken aim at the scoreboard and caused some damage.

I threw up again in the holding cell, then passed out on a bench that would normally have been way too uncomfortable for sleep. I awoke to my father's voice.

"Sam, hey! Get up."

I was slow to react at first. Fuzzy head, bleary eyes, sore body. But I knew the voice that was calling out to me. "Shit. Dad, how did you know I was here?"

"The police called us," he answered. "It's OK for you to leave now. How about we go home?"

"Yeah, I'd like to go home."

The long drive back to my parents' house gave me a chance to unfold the details of the previous day. I was grateful for the confined space of the truck's cab --familiar territory where all kinds of discussions had taken place. Dad wasn't angry about my drunken misadventures, but I could sense his disappointment and hurt at my behavior. And I knew it wasn't just about this incident. Since starting the agency job and moving into my own apartment, I'd barely seen my parents.

"I'm sorry about this," I said, realizing that I had more to apologize for than the police station pickup.

"Are you OK, Sam?" It was a rhetorical question. "You don't seem OK. Look, I know it's upsetting to lose a job. But are there other problems you're dealing with?"

This would have been a good time to acknowledge the practice of functional alcoholism I'd been trying to perfect. But I wasn't ready to step back and comment on the big picture. I took a closer look at the paperwork that I'd been given before being released. "It says here I've got to go to court."

"Yeah, it looks like you have to appear in front of a judge, and you're probably get some sort of sentence or fine."

Shit. "I won't have to go to jail, or anything like that, will I?"

There was a pause before the answer came, and I could sense how sad my father felt about my behavior. "Look, Sam…I'm pretty sure you'll get off with some sort of fine, and maybe some community service. That's what one of the cops told me, anyway. You're just going to have to wait and see."

Chapter 11

Over the next few days, I made several trips between my parents' house and my apartment, gathering up the stuff I'd accumulated during my brief foray into life as a young professional. It didn't feel good to be moving back into my childhood home –a major blow to an ego built around my white-collar ambitions. But the severance payment I'd received wasn't substantial, and my meager savings wouldn't last long paying rent and living expenses in Stamford. Fortunately, my landlady had a waiting list of potential renters for my apartment; it was kind of her to let me break my lease.

My court date arrived a couple of weeks after my arrest. In a unified demonstration of tough love, my parents let me know that they wouldn't be helping me pay for legal representation. I didn't hold this against them. The more I contemplated my drunken escapade, the worse I felt. Yeah, this was a low point. It sure felt strange to put on a jacket and tie, and even stranger to wait in a giant foyer with a scary collection of miscreants and lawyers. The judge who presided during my day in court was a proud supporter of local sports programs, and a regular spectator at different athletic fields, including the one I'd desecrated. He spent a minute or two extolling the beautiful public parts and ball fields in the community, then asked me how I felt about what I'd done.

"I'm ashamed of my behavior, your honor."

"As well you should be, son," he said. "According to the director of recreation, it's going to cost about $1700 to repair the scoreboard you damaged. I want you to pay for this repair. And if I'm not mistaken, you've got some carpentry skills. You and your father rebuilt a deck for a friend of mine about a year ago. I want you to replace the rotten siding on the dugouts at this field, and give these structures a fresh coat of paint. The city will pay for the materials, but you're going to supply the labor."

Yes, you could say I got off easy. The descent back into carpentry work was upsetting, but I consoled myself with the thought that I could get through this spate of community service quickly. I met with the head of maintenance for the city's recreation department, and we put together a list of lumber, fasteners, and finish for the repairs I'd be making. Once all the supplies arrived, it took me two days to get the job done. It was another week before the scoreboard could be repaired, and covering that cost took my bank account down to just over $500.

I needed to get a new job. Unfortunately, there weren't that many advertising agencies in Stamford, Greenwich, and other cities along the I-95 corridor. The opportunities that looked best for me were all in New York, and it was a major ordeal for me to get into the city. It took close to an hour for me to drive from my parent's home to the Stamford train station, another 45 minutes for the train ride into Grand Central, and a healthy cushion of time to make my way to an agency's location.

The job search was expensive as well as time consuming. Three weeks passed, packed with emailed resumes, phone calls, and half-a-dozen trips into the city. The evening drinking habit I'd developed while living and working in Stamford came to an end while I was living with my parents, but every journey back home from a job interview included a visit to a bar. I didn't frequent my usual drinking establishments near my old job, in order to avoid the embarrassment of meeting friends or former colleagues. Instead, I found out-of-the-way dives where I could drink in peace. Sometime during this period, I switched from beer to vodka --a faster, more efficient way to ingest the elixir that so effectively dulled the pain and reinforced the illusion that everything would be all right.

Chapter 12

Yes, I was angry about losing my job, and afraid that I wouldn't be able to get a similar position anytime soon. I was also unwilling to step back and look seriously at my relationship to alcohol. My parents couldn't help but notice this meltdown. One morning, after seeing me stumble into the house the night before and slur a greeting before heading up to bed, I got the confrontation I knew was coming.

"Sam, it's not going to work for you to go on like this," my mother began. I knew right away this was a serious situation, because my dad was normally the tougher parent.

"I'm not sure I know what you mean," I said, doing my best to play dumb.

"You've got a problem with alcohol," my dad said. "There's no way to sugarcoat this, Sam. Look, I don't know what's been happening in your life since you got out of school, because we haven't seen you much. But I've seen enough in these last few weeks to know that you're not in a good place."

My mom chimed in, "Sam, I know you don't drink when you're here at home, beyond a glass of wine or beer at dinner." Yeah, she was right about that. "But when you go out, it's a different story. You know it's not normal or healthy to get that intoxicated, right?"

There was only one way to answer. "Yeah, I see your point. I can dial it back," I said. But I was already rationalizing my behavior. After all, there were heavier drinkers than me out there. I'd been hanging out with them on a regular basis.

"What's changed, Sam?" my dad asked. "I mean, you used to be really disciplined about staying in shape. You're not looking that healthy these days."

Ouch. "I guess I've been focused on my career, and on all the social stuff that goes with it," I offered.

"We're worried about you," said my mom.

My dad was ready to get to the bottom line. "Sam, you can stay here while you look for a job, but only if you agree not to come home drunk. That's the agreement we need to make."

"Yeah. OK," I agreed.

"And look, Sam," Mom continued, "I think it would be good if you could get back into exercising and taking better care of yourself. Maybe it would help if you saw a therapist…"

I knew that was too great a leap. "Mom, I'll be OK," I said, "I just need to concentrate on getting a job."

It was mid-morning when we finished talking, and I didn't feel like hanging around the house. I put on a pair of sneakers and went out for a walk. It was a crisp, cool September day –perfect for the longer runs I used to do. At a walking pace, I retraced one of my jogging routes, noting the landmarks that I once used to punctuate my journey: a tree split by a lightning strike but still surviving, a stone wall where I once spied a giant copperhead basking in the sun, a flat rock face where someone had painted an American flag after the 9/11 tragedy. At the time, I wasn't able to explain my sour mood, but from this vantage point, I think I was mourning the loss of fitness and simplicity I'd taken for granted in my earlier life. About 20 minutes into my walk my phone rang and I answered without looking at the name display. I uttered a curt hello, then heard a familiar voice. "Sam, it's Bridget Evans."

"What, who, oh…Mrs. E, I mean Bridget." Yes, I was flustered.

She didn't give me much time to fidget. "Hi Sam. Look, I heard about what happened to you from Grant. I mean about losing your job and getting arrested, and all that."

"Yeah, things haven't been going too well lately," I said.

"That's why I'm calling. I'm sorry you're going through a tough time. I'm not sure what your plans are, but if you've got a minute or two there's a job I have that might interest you."

I stepped off the little side road I was on and leaned back against a tree. "Well, I've been going on job interviews, mostly in the city," I replied. "But I haven't had any luck yet."

After a short pause, she continued. "My family has an old country house up in Cornwall; it's a couple of hour's drive from here. We hardly ever go up there, and the place has deteriorated pretty badly."

"So, you need someone to make repairs? Why don't you just sell the place?" I asked.

"It's complicated," Bridget answered. "The house is part of the historic district, and my family has a history in the town, too. The little public library is named after my great grandfather. The house is still owned by a family trust, but we want to restore it and then donate it to the local historical society."

"Are you offering me a job doing the fix-up work?"

"Yeah, that's the idea. I don't know what your plans are, and I apologize if this is way off base. I know you're good with your hands," she said, with a quick laugh I barely caught. "We need to do something about the place before it really starts to fall apart. If it's something you'd like to do, let me know and we can work out the details."

"I appreciate the offer, Mrs., I mean Bridget. "I'm really hoping to get my career back on track, but I'll let you know if that changes. It's nice to hear from you."

"Good to talk to you, too, Sam."

Chapter 13

Another week passed by, filled with several phone interviews, lots of online applications, and an expensive reworking of my resume by a career counseling service. So far, a month of prospecting had netted me a couple of paid internship offers, but the salaries wouldn't come close to covering an apartment and commuting costs. And speaking of costs, I had less than $200 in my checking account.

On Wednesday of the following week, I headed into the city for what looked like the most promising interview so far. The agency —with the cute but cryptic name of "Rickshaw"-- was small and fairly new. But I was impressed with the major accounts they'd landed, and with their roster of young employees. My interview was scheduled for mid-afternoon, so I started driving to the train station around 10:00. My phone rang just as I pulled into the station's parking lot.

"Is this Sam?" an unfamiliar voice inquired. When I answered, she continued. "This is Mary, from Rickshaw. Sam, I apologize for the last-minute notice, but I'm calling to tell you that we filled the position you were scheduled to interview for."

Shit. "I don't understand." was all I could say.

"OK, well I'm not supposed to tell you this, but Cameron hired his nephew for the job. This just happened yesterday."

"Damn. I thought I would be a good fit with you guys," I said. "It would have been nice to hear this news from Cameron."

"Yeah, you're right," Mary replied. "I feel bad for you. I'm just the messenger. Well, I'm sure you'll land in a good place, Sam. Good luck."

You wouldn't think the day would get worse after that turn of events, but it did. I really tried to find something positive to be thankful for, but the best I could come up with was *Hey, at least I didn't buy my train ticket and waste a trip into New York*. It didn't help that I could see the office building where I used to work as I drove out of town. Yeah, you know what happened next. I headed back toward my parent's house, but stopped at a liquor store on the way. I knew I was making a mistake as I pushed the door open and put a fifth of vodka down on the checkout counter, but I didn't have the power to stop myself.

Planning to get drunk does actually require some important decisions, like where to engage in your favorite activity if you're not going to be in a bar. Thanks to a bit of quick thinking, I remembered a seldom-used parking area adjacent to some hiking trails on the way to my parent's house. I parked as innocuously as possible and turned off the motor, but kept the ignition on so I could listen to the radio while I drank. Maybe there would be news of some terrible disaster or tragedy that would make my problems seem miniscule in comparison. A nice, sensible wish that didn't come true. Instead, I passed out before emptying the bottle of its magical contents.

I was still drunk when I woke up just after 3 in the afternoon. I needed food and some coffee to sober up, but I knew I couldn't drive or call my parents. I finished the rest of the vodka while walking in circles around my car, reasoning that the physical activity would counteract the effect of the booze. Yeah, it actually made sense at the time. Right before I returned to the back seat of my car, I sent a text to my mom, telling her that I would be staying over at a friend's house.

It was dark when I woke up, this time with a wicked headache. I walked around outside, peed in the woods, and decided to risk driving to a nearby gas station to get something to eat. The plan was to get some food and coffee, drive back to my parking spot, and try to sleep off the hangover. I managed to drive to a gas stop a few miles away without incident. A trip to the rest room to splash some water on my face revealed a scary looking character in the mirror. What he said to me was: *How did you fuck this up so bad?*

Chapter 14

The sun was just coming up when I awakened in the back seat and stumbled outside to escape the noxious funk of my alcoholic exhalations. Breathing in some fresh air seemed to alleviate the nausea. I stretched and walked around, noticing the dappling of sunlight through the trees, and the sound of birds in the nearby woods. The cliché of "a new day" popped into my head, but then I registered the foul taste in my mouth, the pain behind my eyes, the cancelled interview and my seemingly futile quest for a new job.

It was too early to drive back to my parent's place. I glanced at the rustic sign next to a path leading into the woods, showing a map of trails and points of interest. This seemed like a good time for a walk, so I started up the path. My first thoughts were of Christina, because I remembered taking long walks together on different nature trails. Our conversations ranged far and wide, driven initially by curiosity about each other, but then by combinations of contemplation, observation, and questions about what our futures had in store for us. I realized with some sadness that I was much happier then. If Christina were here she would have asked "Why do you think that is, Sam?"

My phone pinged after I'd been walking for 10 minutes or so. It was a text from my bank letting me know that my checking account was overdrawn by $43. Shit. That's it, brother. You don't have a savings account so you're officially out of money. Yeah, I knew it was coming. But I kept thinking that I'd land a new job and start rebuilding my collapsed finances. The contemplative spirit I'd been enjoying evaporated, and I headed back to the car. By the time I got there, I was ready to give Mrs. E a call.

She didn't pick up, so I left a message and started to drive home. I got a return call about 5 minutes later, and pulled into a gas station to talk. "Sam, it's good to hear from you," she began. "Listen, I know you weren't feeling optimistic about taking on this carpentry job. I hope you've changed your mind."

"Sure," I lied. "I guess we should arrange to meet up at your property," I said.

PART 3

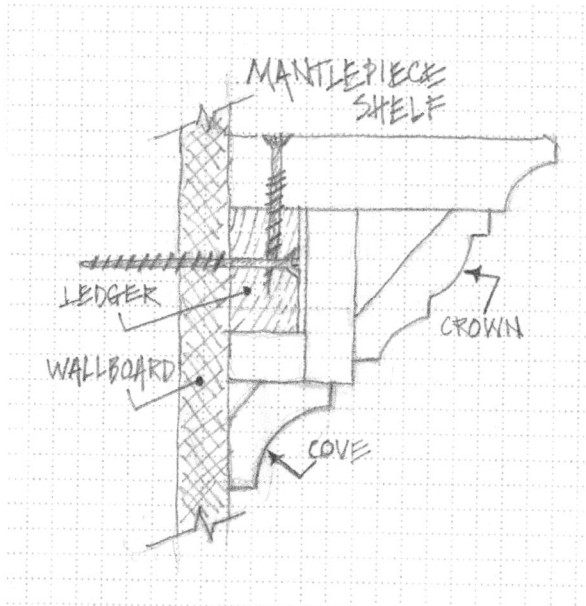

Finish. to bring (something) to an end or to completion; complete: to finish a project; to finish breakfast. (CONSTRUCTION) applied material –such as paint, varnish and molding—whose purpose is to protect and/or beautify.

Chapter 15

I arrived in Cornwall on the second Monday in August. The day was clear but cool, offering a mild preview of autumn's arrival. My car was packed: work boots and flannel shirts on the floor in the front, the back seat occupied by a suitcase full of clothes, a backpack with my laptop and a couple of notebooks, and all kinds of carpentry tools in the trunk. On the drive up, I realized that the end of my affair with Mrs. E had been almost exactly six years ago. How strange to be getting back together in such an unexpected way.

It was easy to spot my destination. The antique, Colonial-style home known as Curtis House seemed out of place next door to a small elementary school, in a neighborhood of modest ranch houses. The tiny town center I'd driven through to get here was quaint and vastly different from the chain restaurants, fast food franchises, and megastores that blanketed the landscape two hours south. I noticed a small grocery store, a post office, and an Agway store on my way in, along that other essential, a liquor store.

I'd talked with my parents about taking Mrs. E up on her offer, and I knew my dad was hurt that I didn't want to simply rejoin him, teaming up on remodeling jobs like we used to. But I couldn't stand the idea of returning to work for wealthy families I'd known through school. I was still aiming to work my way into that upper crust. This was just a brief return to carpentry until I could get back on my feet financially, and I was doing it in an out-of-the-way location to avoid embarrassing encounters.

Curtis House had once been a fine example of a New England center-hall Colonial. It had the classic centered chimney, and a symmetrical front façade with a large door framed by fluted molding and an ornate pediment. I noted the granite steps and the stone foundation. The local historical society had erected a plaque alongside the entry path, providing interesting historical details. I figured out that Jackson Curtis, the original owner and town benefactor, must have been the family member Mrs. E had referred to in our conversation.

I took out a small note pad and started to write down repairs that members of the historical society might want me to make: missing and damaged clapboards, old windows, rotten exterior trim, deteriorated mortar…It was a lot worse than I could have imagined. I didn't have the experience or expertise to take on some of this work. I wrote a few question marks down for work that would need to be done by subcontractors, then heard Mrs. E's car pulling into the driveway.

There was an awkward moment when she got out of her SUV. Uncertain about the greeting I needed to make, I reached out to shake hands. "Oh Sam," she said, "give me a hug. It's good to see you. And if you call me Mrs. E, I'm going to punch you."

After a few moments exchanging some token family news, we turned toward the house. "So, what do you think?" she asked.

"Gosh, Bridget, there's a lot of work to do here," I answered.

"Yes," she said. Then I watched as she looked up at the house and glanced at the surrounding landscape. She seemed to be reminiscing about the place, momentarily unaware of my presence. And in those few moments, I did some reminiscing of my own, thinking about the time we spent together in the summer before I started college. She had aged in 6 years, but I didn't think she was any less beautiful.

"Yes," she repeated. "Let's take a look inside. I see you've already started making some notes."

"Yeah, well I think the best thing to do is make a list of all the repairs that need to be done. Then we can prioritize the work. As I spoke these words, trying to sound professional, I realized I was channeling my dad, an involuntary reflex based on numerous customer interactions I'd observed in the past.

Bridget nodded. "That's a good idea. I asked Pete Bromley to come by. I'd like you to meet him. He's a retired builder who has been here forever. He's also a member of the local historical society. I know Pete's looking forward to working with you."

"OK, sounds good." That was all I could muster, because most of my attention was on the interior details I was seeing. The entry foyer had wide board flooring that I guessed to be oak or chestnut.

The wood needed refinishing but was in fairly good condition. The newel post at the bottom of the main stairway wobbled badly when I took hold, and some of the treads were dished from years of use. As I added to my notes, I noticed musty smell, prompting me to ask when the place was last lived in.

"Well, we had a caretaker who lived here up until last year some time," Bridget answered. "There's a little apartment in the back I'll show you. I was assuming that's where you could stay, if you don't want to make the long drive back and forth to your folks' place."

We eventually reached the living space, after inspecting the basement and all the other rooms. Along the way, my repair list had grown to intimidating size. I was fighting off some intense depression –not just because of the amount of work to be done, but also due to the realization of how far I'd deviated from the script I'd been counting on for such a long time. I wanted a drink badly.

The caretaker's apartment was located in a shed-roofed addition at the back of the house. It turned out to be nicer than I'd anticipated –small, but well looked after, with its own bathroom and older but functional appliances. OK, I could probably stay here, I reasoned. It was rent-free accommodation, which certainly would help me get back on my feet financially. But like I said, it was pretty far off the script. Bridget and I headed back outside, and her phone rang just as we got there. I guessed it was Pete Bromley, letting Bridget know he'd be a bit late. "Not a problem," I heard Bridget say. "We're going to head over to Paulette's Café for coffee. Why don't you join us there?"

The little eating establishment was just off Main Street, distinguished by a striped awning that sheltered a couple of outdoor tables and chairs. During the short drive into town, I managed to snap out the daze I'd been in, and realize that we had a bunch of details to work out: how much and how I'd be paid, where I'd order building materials, whether I'd be able to contact and negotiate with subcontractors, and what kind of time frame would be expected. Bridget sensed my anxiety, and –to her credit-- it seemed like she had anticipated many of my concerns.

"Sam, I can understand if this all seems a bit overwhelming," she began, after we'd settled down with our coffees at one of the outdoor tables. "I want to keep things as simple and straightforward as possible, so you can just concentrate on doing a good job, and –I hope—get some satisfaction out of managing the project."

The salary Bridget proposed was good, but not great. Well, I'm not working in Greenwich, I reasoned. And I was pretty desperate to get out of debt. My parents had started paying my health and car insurance bills, but they made it clear that this was only a short-term solution. Bridget explained that she'd forego mailing checks in favor of direct deposit into my depleted checking account. She also reassured me that the utilities for the apartment would be covered by the historical society, an arrangement she'd already worked out.

"What about the building materials I'll need to order, and the other contractors we'll need to do some of the work?" I asked.

"That's what I was hoping Pete Bromley could explain," she answered. He's —oh, look, here he comes," she said, nodding her head towards a tall guy who had just rounded the corner and was walking toward us. Flannel shirt, baseball cap, blue jeans. He looked to be in good shape for his age, which I guessed to be mid-60s. We got through the introductions quickly, with Pete insisting that I call him by his first name. I took a quick glance at my notebook, still worried about all the work that needed to be done.

"Where do you go for building materials around here?" I asked.

"There's a place a few miles north of town," Pete replied. "Lloyd's Lumber. It's not Home Depot, but they've got most of the lumber and supplies you'll need. And they can order other things like windows, doors, and cabinets."

"The historical society has an account with Lloyd's; isn't that right, Pete?" Bridget added.

"Right," he replied. "You'll need to hold onto the receipts so I can keep the accountant happy. I'd also like you to talk with me about any big-ticket items you need. I'll take you up there and introduce you to the Lloyd's crew. Do you have a truck?"

"Not anymore. Do they make deliveries?"

"Yes, although you might need to wait a while. I've still got an old pickup I could lend you. When do you think you'll get started?"

"I'll gather my tools and stuff over the weekend. Why don't I give you a call when I get here on Monday? Is that OK for a start date, Bridget?"

"Sure," she replied. "The sooner, the better."

After we exchanged phone numbers, Pete excused himself, leaving Bridget and I at the table. It seemed like we'd covered all the details I needed to get started. I was about to thank Bridget for the opportunity and the coffee when she asked the question I had been too afraid to pose: "Do you ever think about that summer we spent together?"

"I do, actually," I replied. After pausing for a moment, I said "It kind of messed me up for a while when I got to college. I, uh….It's hard to explain, but I think that it caused some confusion as I tried to have relationships with girls at school. I don't know if that makes sense…" Yeah, I was still confused.

"Sam, I understand," she said. "You're a good person, and you deserve to find someone your own age, or close to it, anyway, who can be a soulmate. I'm sorry if I got in the way of that."

"It's OK. I mean, I don't regret the time we spent together," I offered. "And you got a great pool house, after all."

She laughed. "You're right, Sam. Look, I'm sure everything will work out well for you. I'm really glad to have you in charge of this restoration project."

Chapter 16

I was grateful to my dad for holding onto all my carpentry gear. I knew he did so in hopes that we'd be able to work together again, but I think he understood why I decided to choose an out-of-the-way location to make my re-entry into manual labor.

Talking over some of the details with my dad countered some of the job's overwhelming aspects, but it didn't alter my bad attitude about the place I'd come to. Although I made a good show of being positive in front of my parents, I spent the weekend in a foul mood, envisioning this return to carpentry work as a troublesome obstacle I'd need to overcome in order to get back on the right path. My funk had deepened when I realized that I wouldn't have internet access in the apartment at Curtis House; the closest wifi would be at Paulette's Café or the local library. I'd learned that cell phone reception was pretty spotty, too. Yes, I had the starring role in a movie about life out in the sticks. The low point of the weekend is easy to remember. I decided to go for a run, just like I used to do when something was bothering me. But less than mile along, I was so out of breath from being so out of shape that I had to stop and turn back. No one was around to see me crying as I asked myself *What the fuck are you doing?*

Pete's truck was parked in front of Curtis house when I arrived on Monday–an old Dodge that looked to be in nice condition despite its age. I found him around the side of the house, in front of a small building that might have been a carriage house years ago. Pete was wearing the same clothes he'd had on for our first meeting, plus a pair of worn work gloves. We exchanged greetings, and I remarked on the condition of his vehicle.

"When I stopped the full-time carpentry work, I decided to fix up the old truck. It gets me a few compliments now and then."

"My old Tacoma would be useful about now," I commented.

"Hey, I wouldn't worry about that. You can borrow this beast when you need to haul something," Pete said. "I've got a Honda Civic I used as my daily driver." He glanced over at the outbuilding. "I wanted to give you a hand cleaning this out. This place hasn't been used much for a long time, but you'll be storing tools and materials here, so most of this junk can get thrown out. I've got a dumpster coming later this morning, but we can start to sort through this stuff now."

By the time the dumpster arrived 45 minutes later, we had separated the good from the bad, cleared away a small galaxy of cobwebs, and created a generous amount of open space inside the building. Pete proposed a drive up to the lumber yard, with a stop for lunch on the way back. It seemed like a good idea. "Let's go in my truck, if you don't mind," he proposed. "If you pull into the yard in that Camry of yours, I'm afraid your credibility will suffer."

"Agreed," I answered, then posed a question. "Pete, do you think it would be OK for me to add a couple of extra lights and an electrical outlet in the shed? I'll probably end up doing some cutting and assembly work out there, so the extra outlets would be helpful."

"That sounds like a good idea. I know an electrician you can call."

"I think I can do that little amount of wiring on my own," I said. "I learned how to do some basic electrical work from my dad."

"Sounds like he taught you well, son."

The trip to Lloyd's Lumber was a pleasant surprise. There aren't too many independent lumber yards left anywhere, and despite its rural location, this family-owned business seemed to be doing well. When I wondered aloud about this success, Pete explained that that this little corner of Connecticut had a history of attracting wealthy New Yorkers who wanted a second home in the country. "I've had plenty of clients over the years who just come up from the city a few times a year. But they always find something to upgrade, replace or repair," he said.

As he drove, Pete pointed out different houses where he'd done a wide variety of work over the years. When we passed a large,

Victorian-style place set back from the road, Pete said "I'll never forget the time I did a complete kitchen makeover for the city couple who bought that place. Less than six months after I completed the job, they sold the house to other New Yorkers who hired me to tear out the cabinets I'd installed and do everything over in a different style."

"Wow!" was all I could manage to say in reply to Pete's story. When we got to Lloyd's Lumber, Pete introduced me to the crew there, explaining that I'd be handling the repair and restoration work on Curtis House. I had the feeling that his endorsement meant a lot. The only snag in my visit was an embarrassing mistake I made with the forklift operator.

When we entered the main warehouse at the back of the yard, Pete pointed at the forklift and said "That must be Jessie." For a couple of minutes, Jessie seemed oblivious to our presence. We just watched as he maneuvered the machine to deftly grab the topmost pallet from a tall stack, lift it free, and then lower the load while backing up at the same time. The only thing that wasn't impressive was the way Jessie tossed what looked to be a spent roll of tape towards a trash can in a nearby corner, missing the target by a big margin. It was cool inside the building, and I saw that Jessie had dressed for the occasion, sporting a bulky sweatshirt and a thin wool cap.

Pete made a quick introduction, and I complimented Jessie on the forklift performance, but added with a chuckle "But that trash can toss was lame, Jessie. You kinda throw like a girl."

The reply came quickly: "Yeah, I get that a lot." Then when the cap came off and I took a second look at my new acquaintance, I realized I was looking at a woman about my age or a little older. She had short, straight brown hair, with green eyes and a sprinkling of freckles across her nose. *Shit.*

"Damn, Jessie. I thought..."
"Yeah, I know. Don't sweat it," she answered. "I've heard worse."

Luckily, Pete stepped in to help limit my embarrassment, explaining restoration initiative at Curtis House. "Sam's going to be a familiar face around here, I'm afraid. The place needs a lot of work.

Jessie agreed. "It sure does. I live in the same neighborhood, and I drive by the place when I drop my son off at school. It's been painful to see the property so neglected. Sam, if there's something you can't figure out, just ask Pete. He's the best carpenter I know."

Pete thanked Jessie for the compliment, and I said "I think I'm going to need all the help I can get."

Chapter 17

During the drive back to Curtis House, I got to know a little more about Pete's background. It surprised me to learn that he grew up in a wealthy family and attended a private school that was a rival of Kirkland. The Vietnam War was going on when he graduated, and Pete got drafted.

"I thought about dodging to Canada," he said, "but I ended up spending two years in country, working with Army engineers to keep airfields operable. When I got back stateside, I jumped on the fast track as a salesman for a big auto parts distributor. I traveled all over the Northeast, wining and dining store owners and parts suppliers. I ran my life at top speed because I didn't want a spare moment to think about my time in the jungle. But then I crashed and burned pretty badly. Had to come up here and make a fresh start."

When I shared about the events that led to this temporary retreat from my corporate career, Pete just raised his eyebrows and said "Well, it looks like you've got a fresh start opportunity, too."

That first day on the job up in Cornwall had gone pretty well, mainly because Pete had been around to get me started and keep me focused on the project. But when he dropped me back at Curtis House and I was alone with my own thoughts, it didn't take long for me to get into a bad place. I stopped thinking about carpentry and started to think about the big picture –being stuck in a small town where I didn't know anybody, working by myself on a house full of problems.

I made a trip to the grocery store to buy food and a few other essentials. What I didn't need to do was stop at the liquor store. But you know how it is. The loneliness of my situation hit me pretty bad, and I dealt with it in a predictable way. I didn't even wait to unload my groceries before popping open my first can of beer and taking a generous slug of vodka. I was drunk by the time my pizza came out of the oven.

The weather got colder over the next couple of weeks. During that time, I filled the dumpster with a mix of damaged building materials. There were old skirtboards and clapboard siding that needed to be replaced, plus the plumbing fixtures, tile, plaster and rotten framing material from an upstairs bathroom we had agreed to rebuild. I also had to clear out a bunch of miscellaneous debris from the basement and attic. It was messy work, but I had mentally prepared for it, remembering that the initial destructive phase of renovation is always more discouraging than the constructive phase that follows.

It takes discipline and a strong constitution to maintain the habit of functional alcoholism. I never drank on the job. Instead, I simply repeated the pattern I'd developed while I was working at the ad agency. The main difference was that I didn't need to drive to a bar for my after-work buzz. I'd simply take off my tool belt, and head back to the apartment for my medication. The evening alcohol consumption, combined with the fatigue that accrued after a day of manual labor, made for an early bedtime. In the morning, I'd stumble into the apartment's tiny kitchen, down a tall glass of water, then dose myself with strong coffee and a big bowl of cereal.

Several days a week, I'd go to Paulette's Café for lunch. After putting in my order, I'd take my laptop over to a corner table and grab the wifi signal to check my email. The constant banter between customers and the café crew provided interesting snippets of small-town life, but made it impossible to do any serious email correspondence. I stopped following up on job openings I found online. Making time for phone interviews was difficult, and there was no easy way –time or money-wise-- to get into the city from this distant location. There was another reason, too; I just didn't want to acknowledge it at the time. I'd fallen into a rut of my own making, living with a low level of daily depression that I could easily maintain through each evening's alcohol infusion.

Pete made good on his offer to lend me his truck, which I used to pick up new siding, synthetic skirtboards, and other materials. He also put me in touch with an HVAC contractor to assess the heating system, and a basement waterproofing specialist who could hopefully solve the building's wet basement problem. Connecting me with the local trades was hugely helpful. I didn't have the expertise or tools to take on certain renovation tasks, and Pete had an impressive roster of tradespeople he'd worked with over the years. Most of the hands-on work I'd be doing were carpentry repairs. But I'd also be responsible for getting bids that Pete could present to the board. Once the work was OK'd, I'd schedule the contractor, and handle any demo, cleanup, and reconstruction necessary to complete the job. The plumber we ended up using was a father-and-son team; so was the arborist we hired to take down a couple of dead trees on the property. Seeing these two generations working together reminded me a lot of my dad and me.

Pete was helpful in other ways, too. There's never just one way to do something in carpentry. Whenever he stopped by, Pete would always have some tips and tricks to pass on. He showed me a nifty jig for holding one end of a long clapboard in place so I could mark the opposite end for an exact fit against a corner board or window casing. "Never measure when you can mark," he advised.

Pete liked to stop by early in the morning, on his way to meet friends for breakfast at the senior center. At first, I didn't think he noticed the mildly hungover state that I experienced as part of my morning routine. But he called me on it a couple of weeks into the job.

"Do you have a problem with alcohol, Sam?"

Wow, that's direct. But I had a good comeback ready. "Hey, I have a few beers at the end of the day," I lied. "It's not a big deal."

"I'm not judging you, Sam," Pete replied. "I'm just calling it as I see it."

It was time to change the subject. "Pete, that little block plane you lent me is worth its weight in gold. I've been using it to ease sharp edges and fine-tune the fit of clapboards and trim. Where can I get one?"

Pete smiled. "You can't. Stanley stopped making that model decades ago. But you can use that for as long as you want. Tools aren't meant to sit idle. I'll loan you some sharpening stones to keep the blade sharp."

"Thanks," I said. The truth was that even in the short amount of time I'd been working on the house, Pete's advice had been hugely helpful. When I wasn't sure where the sweet spot was between practicality and historical authenticity, I'd come to count on this retired carpenter for the right solution.

Chapter 18

On weekday mornings, a bunch of kids would run, skip, and cavort across the sidewalk in front of Curtis House, on their way to the nearby elementary school. There was a steady congestion of cars, too, aiming for the same destination. I got in the habit of coming outside to enjoy this parade of energy, innocence and brightly colored backpacks. It was as much of a hangover cure as the strong coffee I brewed every morning. I'd sometimes be able to spot Jessie in her Subaru wagon, driving her son to school. I'd had a little more interaction with her and other folks at Lloyd's Lumber as I showed up to order or pick up materials, and I'd gotten to know some employees a little better. It turned out that I had competed against a friend of one of yard crew guys in a state track meet back in high school. And I learned that Jessie's son, Shawn, was 10 years old and had Down Syndrome. I knew a little about this condition from my mom, and from a classmate who had a Down Syndrome sibling. I knew it wasn't easy to raise a child with mental retardation, so I asked Jessie how Shawn was doing in school.

"Shawn likes his special ed teacher," Jessie said. "and she's good about communicating with me, which I appreciate."

"How well is he able to talk?" I asked. "I learned a little about Down Syndrome from my mom, who's a teacher. I've only spent time with one Down Syndrome kid, and I remember that she couldn't verbalize very well."

"It's a challenge," Jessie replied. "Shawn has a pretty good vocabulary –you know, everyday words. But he can't form sentences very well. I can usually understand what he's trying to say. Judy Emory –that's his special ed teacher—she's pretty good at it, too."

As she was talking, I reviewed my memories of Carrie, the Down Syndrome girl I'd met back in high school. A wave of sympathy for Jessie washed over me as I recalled listening to Carrie's mom talk about the difficulties she encountered, and about how much we take for granted –that babies will be healthy and normal, and grow into regular kids. I didn't want to mess things up by saying something stupid like "I'm sorry." So instead I latched on to something positive. "Well, it sounds like Shawn is lucky to have such caring parents."

I saw a smirk sneak onto Jessie's face. "Yeah, that's true for one parent, anyway. My husband couldn't handle having a son who wasn't normal. He lives in Atlanta. We got divorced before Shawn's first birthday."

Shit. "Wow, that's too bad, Jessie."

Her reply came quickly. "Not really. Depending on a guy just seems to get me in trouble. I've learned my lesson. Shawn and I are doing OK on our own." Was that a trace of bitterness I detected in her tone? Yeah, maybe this little bit of history explains the hard edge I'd encountered in my brief interactions with her.

"Who takes care of him while you're at work?" I asked.

"I can usually drop him off at school in the morning, on my way to work. We live pretty close to the school, so he usually walks home on his own. I have Louisa to take care of him in the afternoon. She doesn't charge me much, and she really cares for Shawn."

Chapter 19

It wasn't difficult to settle into a lazy weekend routine, once I'd moved into the apartment at Curtis House. On some Saturdays, I'd need to be available to meet with subcontractors who were too busy to stop by during the week. I found an electrician who could replace all the old incandescent lighting with more efficient LED lights, while making sure to reuse antique light fixtures or find new equivalents that would be historically appropriate. Pete put me in touch with a millwork shop that still had a small supply of picture rail molding to replace some original pieces that had been damaged. He also found me a painting contractor who could show me how to safely strip lead paint from interior trim.

Apart from the weekend appointments with other trades guys, I was free to sleep late, have a leisurely lunch at Paulette's Cafe, and park myself in a comfortable chair at the library where I'd read magazines for a couple of hours. At some point over the weekend, I'd drive down to see my parents. We'd usually plan for dinner on Saturday or lunch on Sunday. I know these visits meant a lot to them, but they were difficult for me. Mom and Dad knew better than others how determined I had been to gain entrance to the white-collar world. I never did a good job of faking enthusiasm for the carpentry work I was doing.

My choice of drinking establishments in Cornwall was pretty limited. The bar at Greenbrier's –the town's only restaurant— couldn't seat more than six people. Driving about 20 minutes south brought me to a dive frequented by a scary group of locals. Neither place seemed like a comfortable place to drink. I was afraid of the local gossip that might accrue if I became a regular at Greenbrier's, and leery about driving drunk on my way back from the dive bar. So that was my rationale for abusing alcohol in the confines of Curtis House. I'd sometimes wander around the old rooms with drink in hand, having imaginary conversations with Jacob Curtis about his horny descendant or his Civil War exploits. Most of the furniture had been put into storage to facilitate repair work, but there was an old couch in the sitting room where I passed out a couple of times.

Bridget called every week or so to check up on my progress. I knew she was talking to Pete on a regular basis, so her calls to me weren't really necessary. She seemed less concerned about the restoration work, and more interested in what I thought about Cornwall. "It's a nice little town, don't you think?" she asked, after mentioning a few local attractions. I tried to respond positively, covering up how lonely and out of sorts I felt most of the time.

A smarter, healthier person would have made the effort to stay in touch with friends and former coworkers. But I'd made a deliberate choice to avoid contact in the immediate aftermath of my arrest, and I'd let these connections lag for so long that I wasn't sure how to go about renewing them. Besides, I thought to myself, do I really want my former colleagues and classmates to know what I'm doing now? As it turned out, they found out anyway. It happened on Columbus Day, a holiday that I'd totally forgotten about. On that Monday afternoon, I was up on a ladder, painting the trim around a window, when Grant Evans pulled up in front of the house in a big SUV.

"Hey, Sam!" he yelled. I recognized his voice, and also the three friends who came with him. Taken by surprise, I wasn't able to say anything in reply. I did a minimal wave with the hand that was holding the paintbrush, and began an awkward descent.

We greeted each other with a combination of handshakes, hugs, and fist bumps. It must have been obvious how awkward I felt about this surprise visit, but Grant wasn't deterred. "Dude, don't you know it's a holiday? You ought to be taking the day off."

"Columbus Day. Yeah, it totally escaped me. I never expected to see you up here," I said.

"My mom keeps saying how nice and quaint it is. We were bored with the scene back home, so I suggested a field trip. How about taking the afternoon off and showing us the sights?"

I forced a smile. Yeah, I thought. We can stop by Lloyd's Lumber and the liquor store, my two major points of interest. I did some quick thinking, then suggested the state park a few miles down the road. "It's got some hiking trails and a bunch of waterfalls," I offered.

"Sounds great," Grant answered. "But first, why don't you show us what you're doing with the house? I remember coming up here and seeing this place a long time ago, but I think it was in a lot better shape back then."

Apart from Pete and the subcontractors who had been through the house, I'd had no visitors. It was strange to hear a bunch of footsteps and voices echo through the empty rooms. I pointed out half-a-dozen partially completed jobs: piles of old wallpaper in a bedroom where more steaming and peeling needed to be done, an upstairs bathroom stripped of its plumbing fixtures, a frame-and-panel door I'd removed from its opening in order to reglue separated joints. Taking this unexpected tour of the project made me realize what a half-assed job I was doing. I was pretty sure my visitors didn't recognize this scattershot approach as a sign of poor workmanship, but I did. It occurred to me that my dad would be upset if he saw this disorganized jobsite. I did my best to pay attention to the questions that Grant, Steve, Louis, and Craig were asking, but the thoughts going through my head were disturbing.

Grant insisted on including a visit to the apartment in the tour, despite my efforts to dissuade him. I didn't want anyone to see the trash can full of empty beer and vodka bottles, the pile of dirty laundry next to the bathroom door, and the overall mess I'd made.

I got the response I was expecting: "Damn, Sam…you're gonna need to clean up your act if you want to bring a babe back here." Right.

Looking back on this October afternoon, I remember the brightness of the low autumn sun and the breathtaking, multi-colored vista of fall colors at their peak. Unfortunately, I also remember the feelings of shame and embarrassment that overwhelmed the natural beauty and friendship I might have enjoyed. I changed into better clothes, and we all crammed into his SUV for the drive to Kent Falls State Park, where we had ourselves a serious hike. It was close to 4:30 when we piled back into the car, and the guys insisted on stopping at Greenbrier's for drinks and munchies before heading back home. I mumbled a neutral response to the plan, but my visitors weren't having it. "Come on, Sam," Craig insisted. "It's our treat. That hike you took us on is worth a few beers at the very least."

Chapter 20

I didn't stop drinking when they dropped me back at Curtis House. In fact, I really tied one on. Listening to these guys talk about their advancing careers and their fast-paced social lives triggered a major dose of jealousy. I wanted what they had, and that objective seemed hopelessly far away. It took more booze than normal for me to knock myself out. I was still passed out at nine the next morning when Pete shook me awake.

"Get up, Sam. Jesus, you're drunk," he said, jostling me awake.

"Guilty," was all I could muster before stumbling to the bathroom. The simple act of sitting up was all it took to trigger the nausea. For a few minutes, the intense physical discomfort was all I could think about. But once my stomach emptied and I splashed some cold water on my face, I came out of the bathroom to face the emotional damage I'd done to myself and Pete. "I'm sorry, Pete," I said.

"Sam, why don't you get dressed, and we'll go have some breakfast."

When I offered a lame "I'll be OK," Pete just shook his head and said "Put some clothes on. I'll wait for you out front."

I assumed we'd be going to Paulette's Café, but Pete headed north out of town. I didn't know what to say and I still felt like shit, so I just watched the road. When we got to Route 7, a road sign indicated that the Massachusetts border was just 10 miles away.

Pete broke the silence. "There's a diner up the road where I used to be a regular. It's been around a long time, since before the major highways started to siphon traffic off of Route 7." Pete paused for a few seconds. I watched him wet his lips and open his mouth to say something, only to stop himself. Then the words came. "I'm an alcoholic, Sam. I haven't picked up a drink in 28 years, but the urge is still there. "

For once, I didn't feel like making excuses, so I just stared ahead. Pete continued. "Seeing the struggle you're going through reminds me of my ordeal when I was just a few years older than you are now. But it was a lot worse, because I dragged a wife and child through my drunken world."

"God, Pete, I never would have guessed. That's painful to hear."

"It's still painful for me all these years later," he said. "And Sam, I can't bear to see you heading down the same road I was on. When we get done with breakfast, there's an AA meeting at the old Elks Lodge down the road from the diner. I'd like you to go with me."

"AA, you mean Alcoholics Anonymous?" I asked.

"Yeah, that's right Sam. This may not be what you want to hear, but getting sober isn't something you can do on your own. There's no shame in asking for help with an addiction. And if you ask, you'll get it."

Our conversation continued as we pulled into the diner's parking lot. I knew about AA, but I didn't understand why Pete still attended meetings if he hadn't had a drink in 28 years. When I queried him, he smiled and said "That's a logical question to ask, but I'm not sure there's a short answer. I think it's something you'll need to find out for yourself."

The coffee that came soon after we sat down in a booth helped to alleviate the hangover. But my emotional condition wasn't improving. After the waitress left with our breakfast order, Pete said "Look Sam, I need to make something clear. I can see that you're a capable craftsman. It's clear to me that your dad taught you a great deal. But you're managing the project like an alcoholic."

Remembering the revelations I'd had while showing Grant and his buddies around the house, I knew what Pete was talking about. I wanted to acknowledge my agreement, but Pete held up his hand before I could speak. "If you don't clean up your act, I'm going to recommend that we find another project manager."

I couldn't argue with him. In the space of a few seconds, I flashed back to different remodeling projects I'd done with my dad that had brought praise and recognition for good work. I'd lost touch with that feeling of job satisfaction. I realized that Pete was waiting for a response. "You're right, Pete," I agreed.

Pete saw me looking at my watch, and said "Hey, don't worry about the time. The meeting doesn't start for another hour. There's more to talk about, Sam."

"Yeah, I've been trying to figure out what to do with the attic's pull-down stair," I said. "It was obviously added long after the house was built, and it looks really out of place, historically speaking."

"Hey, let's leave that till later," Pete responded. "What I want to know, Sam, is this: What are you fighting? It's clear you're dealing with a drinking problem, and believe me, I know what that's like. But there's something else, too. You don't seem happy or comfortable here."

Busted. It was clear that Pete had seen through my attempts to feign enthusiasm for the project. I felt bad about disappointing him, and I was surprised at the absence of anger or resentment in his tone. I wanted to talk, but I didn't know how to explain the conflicting emotions I had about doing carpentry work –getting praise and good pay from my father, while experiencing feelings of humiliation and inadequacy in front of an audience I wanted to join. I was grateful when Pete filled my silence with his story.

Chapter 21

"My dad was a serious drinker," he began, after signaling the waitress for more coffee. "He took the train into the city every day, to a high-paying job at Chase Manhattan bank. He hung out in the bar car on the way home, and was usually pretty soused by the time he walked in the door."

"Not a good example," I offered.

"It's all relative, Sam. Back in the 60s and 70s, there were plenty of functional alcoholics who held down good jobs. I was luckier than some kids because my dad just got quiet and compliant when he drank. He'd get home late, have a scotch with his dinner, and stumble up to bed. The real loss for me is that I never really got to know the guy. "

I thought about how different my childhood had been. "That's too bad, Pete. My parents are pretty light drinkers. I'm not sure if I've ever seen them drunk. After what you saw your dad go through, how come you…"

"Yeah, I know," Pete replied. "As a kid, you swear that you won't make the same mistakes your parents did. But there I was, conspiring with my high school chums to tap into our parents' liquor supplies. Once I experienced the bravado, euphoria and entertainment value of a good drunk, I didn't want to be without it. There were always a few kids who wanted to get a buzz on."

"That doesn't sound much different from how I grew up," I commented.

Pete nodded his head. "Well, you managed to get through high school with good success as a student and athlete. Sam, you even learned a trade from your dad in the bargain. I got suspended from school not once, but twice. I put my parents through hell. I really believe they were relieved when I got drafted after graduating. I became the army's problem.

"How did you survive over there? I know that a lot of Vietnam veterans came back suffering from PDSD."

"I was luckier than most. For reasons I never understood, they put me with a construction crew that travelled from base to base, rebuilding air strips and damaged barracks. Apart from hunkering down in a bunker during a few mortar attacks, I never saw any combat action. And we were never far from the liquor supply. I wasn't the only lush on my crew."

The Pete I'd been getting to know seemed a long way off from the person Pete was describing. "How did you end up here?" I asked.

"When I got back stateside, I knew I had to clean up my act and leave the war behind. I actually stopped drinking long enough to marry an old high school girlfriend and land a job with a big auto parts distributor. New England was my territory; I travelled to every town and city you could name. We lived in Hamden, so I could hop on I-95 or 91 North within minutes of leaving my driveway."

Pete paused for a few moments to sip his coffee. I wanted to hear the rest of the story. "So, what you're saying is that you were living the dream, at least for a while."

"Yeah, that's about right. My daughter Hannah was born a year after we got married. I was earning a good base salary, plus bonuses when we reached quarterly sales goals. But I had a few store managers who liked to go out for drinks at the end of the day. "C-mon Pete," they'd say, "you can tell me about the new oil filter promotion over a few beers.""

Pete shook his head and blew out a deep breath. I could see a combination of strain and sadness come into his eyes. "Pretty soon drinking with my clients became the rule rather than the exception. It wasn't long before I was keeping a supply of booze in my company car so I could drink anytime and anywhere. I'd even make trips out to the car when I was home."

I wasn't sure I wanted to hear any more of the story. "Pete, I..."

"Sam, just let me finish. Believe me, I'm not giving you the long version of this drunkalogue. –I'll leave out the neglect and alienation of my family and the slow, steady decline of my job performance. What happened was my wife got smart and divorced me. She and Hannah moved in with relatives down in Chapel Hill, North Carolina. I finally hit bottom –that's an AA term—after losing my license on a DUI and getting evicted from my apartment."

"How did you land here?" I asked.

"My parents knew a contractor who was trying to build up business around here. They begged him to take me on. Gene was a recovering alcoholic, so he knew all about my disease. He took me to my first AA meeting, at the Elks Lodge down the road. It wasn't an easy recovery. Hell, I don't think there's any such thing as an easy recovery. Gene and others in the group were always there for me, even when I fell off the wagon. Gene taught me a lot about carpentry, but AA taught me how to live a better life."

"Is he still around?"

"No, he passed back in '89. But I still think of him often. I've got a bunch of the tools he passed on to me, and that old Dodge truck you've been driving used to be his."

"So that's why you've been taking such good care of it," I said.

Chapter 22

"My name is Sam, and I'm an alcoholic." I didn't utter those words during the meeting that Pete and I attended, but I heard a dozen or so others begin their sharing with that acknowledgement. There were also a couple of attendees who identified themselves as addicts rather than alcoholics. I recognized Nick, the HVAC contractor who had done some work at Curtis House, along with a guy I'd seen several times at Paulette's Café, and one of the salesmen at Lloyd's Lumber.

I was surprised to see Jessie at the meeting, and hear her make the same classic introduction. She gave a small nod of recognition when Pete and I entered the meeting room, but otherwise seemed preoccupied. I understood why later in the meeting when she shared about some problems she was having with her son. She talked about confronting the parent of a child who was teasing Shawn on the walk home from school. "He actually accused me of overreacting," she said. "Then he said 'Just because your son's retarded doesn't mean he shouldn't learn how to tolerate a little ribbing.' I got so angry I hung up the phone. If I had any alcohol in the house, I would have drunk it."

I wanted to say hi to Jessie after the meeting, but she left too quickly –probably to get back to her job at the lumber yard. Pete asked me if I wanted to hang around, but I had too many thoughts rattling around in my head to make good conversation, so I told him I'd just like to get back to work. I thought he'd just drop me off when we got back to Curtis House, but he said he'd like to take a look around and assess the work I'd been doing.

We spent nearly an hour going over different work that still needed to be done. Pete started off as I expected he would, reiterating the importance of a neat, well-organized jobsite, and a work plan that didn't leave multiple repairs partially complete. He mentioned that other members of the historical society had expressed interest in seeing how the project was progressing. "I've been holding them off for a while, Sam," he said. "Before I give an informal tour, I need you to get farther along in a couple of places. Pretty soon it will be too cold to work outside, so finish priming the new exterior trim you installed. Then let's focus on a couple of the rooms you've been working on."

I looked at my watch as Pete got ready to leave. It was only a few hours after I had stumbled out of bed, but I was exhausted and overwhelmed by the emotional territory I'd covered, from the story of Pete's early life to all of the sharing I'd heard from different folks at the AA meeting.

We walked into the entry foyer, and I saw Pete pause before reaching for the door handle. He turned around and said, "Sam, this last bit of advice is more important than any renovation details we've discussed. After I leave, you need to dispose of the beer and hard liquor in the apartment, put the place into decent, presentable condition, and get back to the clean slate you had before the alcohol abuse started."

Shit. How long ago was that? In a matter of seconds, I flashed through my earliest experimentation with alcohol, the binge drinking I perfected in college, the after-work boozing I did in Stamford, and the drunken mayhem that landed me in jail after losing my job. Yeah, I knew Pete was right, but the thought of pouring away all that booze seemed extremely wasteful.

Pete must have sensed my reticence. "I'm not going in and helping you with this. It's something you've got to do for yourself, Sam. Think about the way drinking messed up my life, and about the pain and suffering shared in the meeting. There's plenty of support if you want pull yourself out of this addiction, but you've got to take that first step."

"You mean, about admitting I'm powerless over alcohol?" I asked.

"Yeah. That's it. Hold onto that list of meetings I gave you; if you're willing to drive a little ways, you can go to one every day."

"OK Pete. Thanks."

Chapter 23

I spent the rest of the afternoon cleaning up the house, then got the apartment looking better, too. I gathered up a sixpack of beer from the refrigerator and put it in the trunk of my car, not sure about how or if I'd dispose of it. The three inches of vodka that remained in the bottle I stored in the freezer were still too precious to pour down the sink. I finished off the V with my dinner of scrambled eggs and toast. I was buzzed, but not as drunk as I normally would be at this point in the evening. The craving for more alcohol was unmistakable, and it made me feel like shit.

I took a hot shower, hoping it would wash away some of the pain. As I toweled off, the fog slowly cleared from the mirror above the sink, revealing a guy who was out of shape, in need of a haircut, and unable to smile. Thinking about the numerous references to a Higher Power at the AA meeting, I looked upward and asked *How did it get this bad?* I knew the answer. What I said to my reflection was *You dug the hole. Are you ready to climb out?*

I awoke a little earlier than usual the next morning, with a little more clarity, too. It was cold outside, but clear. After a light breakfast, I bundled up in some cold weather running gear, and laced up a pair of running shoes that were stiff and dusty from disuse. I knew I wouldn't get far, or attain anything more than a slow jog, but it was a start. I took what I thought to be a short route, avoiding hills because I knew I couldn't handle them.

There were no mansions fronted by high privacy fences here, like I got used to seeing down in Greenwich. *And what's wrong with that?* I asked myself. Did the people waking up in these modest ranch houses go through the day thinking they're missing out on something bigger and better? About halfway through my jog, I spotted Jessie and her son Shawn in their driveway, getting into her car for the ride to school. I knew they lived in the neighborhood, but wasn't sure where until now. I waved as I jogged by, but Jessie didn't recognize me beneath the wool cap and bulky sweats.

Not long after I got back to the house and showered, Nick showed up to work on the HVAC system. He'd already replaced the ancient oil furnace with a high-efficiency propane unit, but we needed to add a duct run to the apartment. The old wall-mounted electric resistance heater that had been keeping the apartment warm for years was ridiculously inefficient and so dangerous I was surprised the place hadn't burned down. Nick showed me where the new heat register would need to be located, and I cut a right-sized hole in the floor with my Sawzall. As he was packing up his tools, he mentioned seeing me at the AA meeting. I thought I might be in for a long speech about the 12-steps, but he just said "There's some good people there. I try to get to at least one meeting a week."

"How long have you been in AA?" I asked.

"It'll be 6 years on December 15th," he answered. "I got arrested on a DUI. The judge knew I needed to drive in order to do my job, so he didn't take away my license –God bless him. He ordered me to attend at least two meetings a week for 6 months. I thought meetings were a waste of time at first, but showing up was a lot better than losing my license. The thing is, I started to hear other guys tell stories that sounded a lot like mine. That was a wake-up call. I worked up the nerve to ask someone –another guy in the building trades, actually—to be my sponsor. I can't say it's been easy, but living sober is a lot better than what I was doing before."

It was just about noon by the time I cleaned up the small mess we made. I took a few minutes to eat two slices of left-over pizza and an apple, then turned my attention to the upstairs bathroom. Pete understood that the planned gut rehab of the bathroom wouldn't be complete before he brought the board members in for their visit; he just wanted them to see some good progress. I'd already removed the old tile floor and punky subflooring. Now the challenge was to cut large sections of new subfloor to size down in the shed, and tote them up into the bathroom without damaging walls or tumbling down the stairs. It's one of those times you wish for a helper.

It was mid-afternoon by the time I got the last piece of new subfloor glued and screwed in place. The work left me sweaty and tired. When I got downstairs, I undid my tool belt, grabbed an old sweatshirt, and headed outside to cool off and take a short break before beginning my next task. While brushing the sawdust off my pants, I noticed that the daily migration from school to home was taking place. Kids of varying sizes were bundled up in puffy down coats and caps of all colors. As I walked down the gravel driveway to get a little closer to the cacophony of voices, I saw a few older boys tossing little pebbles at a smaller kid whose head was covered by a hood. He was trying to get away, but when he ran forward, it looked like there were other co-conspirators actively blocking his way. Running toward the sidewalk, I heard one of the older kids say "Hey look, the retard's crying."

"Hey, cut that out!" I yelled. "Whoever throws the next stone is gonna be really sorry." I wanted to punch these bullies, but fought the urge, realizing that doing so would have disastrous consequences. But I was still incensed. "You guys should be ashamed of yourselves. Get out of here, I don't want to see you again!"

The band of bullies scattered, and when the little kid looked up at me, I realized who he was. "Shawn, is that you?" As he nodded, I saw a stray tear track down his cheek. "Hey, it's OK, Shawn. I'm

Sam, a friend of your mom's. How about you and I walk home together?"

Shawn nodded again, and as we started walking together, I started to reach for his hand, but thought the better of it, figuring such a gesture would only give the bullies more fodder. Louisa came to the door when we got to Shawn's house; I remembered her name from earlier conversations with Jessie. I explained what happened and she thanked me, saying "Jessie, she tells me about these boys who are hurting Shawn."

"Well, I don't think they injured him," I said, realizing that Louisa was grappling with English as a second language, and probably didn't have "taunting" in her vocabulary. "They're being mean to him for no reason. It really upset me to see Shawn being treated that way."

"Yes, I understand. You are…"

"Sam. Hi. I know Jessie from the lumber yard. She has told me how kind and caring you are with Shawn."

Louisa smiled. "Good to meet you, Sam. You are very nice to look after this little guy."

When I got back to Curtis House, I called the tile guy that Pete had recommended, to let him know we were ready for him to work on the bathroom floor. Then I spent the rest of the afternoon carefully removing the tall baseboard molding in a room where all the original trim had received multiple coats of paint. The plan was to label the trim as I removed it, and take it down to the basement where I would strip off the paint and apply a fresh coat of varnish to restore the natural appearance. Then I'd reinstall the trim, hopefully guided by my labeling system.

I grew anxious as the workday came to an end, because I had been contemplating a quick trip to the liquor store to replenish the supplies I'd deliberately depleted earlier. *Do you REALLY want to keep up with the drinking, Sam?* The answer was yes, but I was grappling with the possibility of changing my behavior. While this internal battle was going on, I opened the refrigerator to evaluate the state of different leftovers. A knock sounded on the back door, and I opened it to find Jessie and Shawn standing there.

"Come on in," I said, startled.

"We didn't come to visit," Jessie said. "Louisa told me what happened when Shawn was walking home from school. We just wanted to stop by and say thanks for intervening. Shawn, do you want to thank Sam for being a good friend today?"

Shawn wasn't wearing his hooded jacket, and I wasn't coping with all the distractions of our earlier encounter, so I got a good look at Jessie's son for the first time. He had short brown hair and the broad face and almond-shaped eyes I knew were common characteristics of Down Syndrome individuals. He smiled at me and said "Tanks, Sam." Then he held out his hand.

I squatted down to reduce the difference in our heights before shaking his hand, and said "No problem, Shawn. I hear you're doing really well in school. I'll be glad to walk you home any time."

Jessie said "I've asked at work about taking time off to get Shawn back from school, but they're giving me a hard time."

"That's too bad. Look, Jessie, I can walk Shawn home after school," I offered. "In fact, I'd like to. I can't stand the thought of those older kids doing that stuff. I guess that's what you were talking about at the meeting."

"Yeah. I tried talking to the parents of those older kids, but it didn't go well. They just kind of laughed it off and insisted I was making a big deal out of harmless teasing. It makes me really angry."

"I can understand that," I said. While we were talking, Shawn walked over to an old ladder-back chair where my tool belt was hanging, and pulled a small prybar from one of the pouches.

"Shawn, put that back," Jessie ordered.

"Hey, that's OK," I countered. Shawn turned and handed me the tool. "Shawn, what you've got there is a pry bar. I use it sometimes to remove moldings and pull out nails. Come over here and I'll show you."

Shawn walked with me over to the bathroom door, and I wedged the broad blade of the bar between the back of the door casing and the wallboard. "So, if you want to pry this board loose, this is a good way to start," I said, pushing on the bar lightly.

When I looked up at Jessie, she said "We really should be going."

I didn't want them to leave. "Have you guys eaten yet?" I asked. "I've got a big batch of chili that my mom made for me over the weekend. It'll probably go bad before I can eat it all. Why don't you sit down and I'll just nuke a few bowls of this stuff in the microwave?"

I could tell Shawn was interested in my offer, but I couldn't get a read on Jessie. She started to answer: "Well,.."

"Look, I never get visitors, unless they're here to do work. And I usually never have food that's this tasty." Was I begging? Yes. "What do you say, Shawn?"

"I like chili."

The kid came through for me. I got my two guests settled around the small table that filled a corner between the kitchen and living room. As I spooned the chow into some bowls, it occurred to me that if I hadn't followed Pete's advice and cleaned up the apartment, this little gathering wouldn't be happening. I nodded a prayer of thanks to my friend.

"What do you guys want to drink?" I asked. "I'm afraid I don't have much of a selection. There are a couple of Diet Cokes in the fridge."

"I like Diet Coke," Shawn said.

"You're not offering me a beer to go with my chili?" Jessie asked.

"Well, I…"

"Take it easy, Sam," Jessie said. "I'm just messing with you. I guess you know I can't drink."

"Uh…yeah. I was surprised to see you at the meeting the other day."

"I've been in AA for a little over 9 years," Jessie said. "I can't go to evening meetings unless I get a sitter for Shawn, so I try to fit in daytime meetings whenever I can. The guy from Lloyd's I came with is the nephew of the guy who owns the business."

"If you don't mind my asking, what made you decide you had a problem?"

Jessie reached over and tousled Shawn's hair, and her son stopped eating long enough to smile at his mom. "It was this guy," Jessie answered. "Shawn was only 8 months old when my husband left. Just a baby. There are a bunch of Down Syndrome characteristics that demand a lot of attention. Diet and a lot of physical therapy stuff. Early intervention, that's what they call it. It's helpful but also exhausting. When I put Shawn to bed at the end of the day, I'd have a couple of glasses of wine to unwind. Pretty soon it was a bottle. Then I'd add a shot or two of hard stuff."

In my imagination I could hear Pete saying "Does this sound familiar, Sam?"

Jessie continued after I handed her a bowl of chili from the microwave. "Early one morning –around 2am or so—I woke up to Shawn screaming in pain. He'd got a foot wedged between the rungs of his crib and he couldn't get loose. I could tell he'd been caught like that for a long time because his ankle was black and blue and bleeding. I'd just passed out as I usually did and slept through the early cries of distress."

"Jesus, Jessie. That's a painful wakeup call."

"Sure was. Until Shawn's ankle healed, I was terrified someone would find out and I'd lose him because of neglect or abuse. I went to my first meeting later that week."

"And you haven't had a drink since then?" I had to ask.

"No, I can't make that claim," she answered. "I had a try or two at controlling my drinking, but I always ended up in the same place. Wow, this chili is good. So how about you, Sam? What's your story? I'm sure Pete didn't bring you to that meeting just for fun."

I should have known that was coming. I wasn't really prepared
to discuss my relationship to alcohol. But hearing someone else
honestly address their faults gave me some reassurance about
doing the same. "I was living down in Stamford, working at an
advertising agency. I lost my job when the company restructured,
and went a little crazy. I got arrested for drunk and disorderly
conduct, and for damaging public property."

"OK, well at least you didn't hurt yourself or anyone else. I'm
guessing that was your first AA meeting." When I nodded, she
changed the subject, sparing me a discussion of my relationship to
alcohol. "How did you end up at Curtis House?" she asked.

"I ran out of money, so I had to move back in with my parents.
But that wasn't working out well," I said, remembering that one of
the reasons I'd taken this job was to escape their objections to my
drinking. I explained the historical connection between the Evans
family and Curtis House, leaving out the details of my relationship
to Bridget. "I'm still aiming to get a job in the city," I concluded.

"Why do that, Sam? It seems like you've got a pretty good thing
going here. Just about all the carpenters we see at Lloyd's are
ready to retire; there aren't any young guys like you to take their
place."

She had a good point; in fact, Pete had told me the same thing.
But I didn't want to explain the entire script for my future that I'd

been crafting for such a long time. Instead, I just said "I'll keep that in mind."

Chapter 24

Jessie and I exchanged phone numbers, and she called the elementary school to explain that I'd be showing up to walk Shawn home from school. I let Pete know about this interruption of my work day, and he was fine with it. "You can just add a little time at the end of the day, Sam," he said. "You know the right thing to do."

I felt nervous and awkward the first few afternoons I walked Shawn home, mainly because I wasn't sure how well we would be able to communicate. He was a lot more comfortable than I was. When he spied me outside the school entrance, I got a big smile, along with an enthusiastic "Hi Sam." After several days of this, I smiled to myself and wondered just who was suffering from diminished capacity here. There were plenty of times when I couldn't understand what Shawn was trying to say to me about his day at school. But I learned to improve my responsiveness, asking questions to home in on the people or events he was talking about. "Is she a teacher? Is he a friend? Did that happen at lunchtime? Did someone get in trouble?"

I got some help from Shawn's special ed teacher. She came out and introduced herself when I first arrived, and was usually there every afternoon. She'd clue me in to the daily highlights that Shawn might want to talk about on the walk home. She also mentioned Shawn's love for WWE –World Wrestling

Entertainment. "Shawn knows all the characters, and he loves talking about their exploits," she explained.

"That's interesting," I replied. "The WWE corporate headquarters is in Stamford; you can see the building from the highway. One of my high school classmates actually got a job in their marketing department."

Not surprisingly, the older kids who had been tormenting Shawn directed their energy and interest elsewhere. And once they realized that I wasn't the angry, threatening personality that they'd initially encountered, a few of the troublemakers introduced themselves and joined in the conversation that took place as we walked.

Jessie made it a habit to call me every evening to thank me for escorting her son. I told her the daily calls weren't necessary, but the truth was I enjoyed hearing from her. I hadn't had a drink since the day Pete took me to the AA meeting, but evenings were still difficult without alcohol. Talking to Jessie made it easier. We would sometimes laugh about Shawn's talent for imitating different people –his uncanny ability to exaggerate notable characteristics and mannerisms like facial expressions or body language. As Shawn grew more comfortable around me, he showcased this talent on a number of occasions. When I mentioned it to Jessie, she explained that Shawn compensated for his limited verbal ability by mimicking people to explain feelings and situations. "Like a lot of parents of Downs kids, I started out using sign language with Shawn," she explained. "We still do it sometimes, but he keeps getting better at talking, which is great."

Little snippets of Jessie's personal history emerged as we talked. I learned that she'd grown up in Cornwall and moved away when she got married, only to move back again after her husband left. "I came back to live with my parents after Bobby left," she explained, "but they moved to Florida when my dad retired. I was hoping to take advantage of some free daycare, but it only lasted a few months."

I also learned a bit more about Jessie's job at the lumber yard. She actually knew a lot about construction, and usually enjoyed the variety of tasks in a given day. In the minus column, she'd had to endure sexist remarks and behavior from customers and fellow employees. "I picked up a drink at the company Christmas party near the end of my first year on the job," she said. "Big mistake. I ended up having a one-night stand with a coworker. It didn't take long for that news to spread around, and bring on all kinds of humiliating comments. Fortunately, the guy no longer works at Lloyd's, and now there's plenty of other gossip for my coworkers to obsess about. But there are still customers who come in and creep me out with endearing names. Do me a favor, Sam, and never call me babe, honey, darling, or anything like that."

"So noted," I replied. Despite (or because of?) Jessie's bad experiences with men, I found myself developing feelings for her. That's a good thing, you might say. But I wasn't familiar with the caring and affection I felt. How could I be, given the fleeting relationships I'd had with women during and just after college? So, while I recognized that something different was going on, it confused and scared me. *Don't get all worked up, amigo. You're probably just lonely and grateful for friendship with someone around your own age. Maybe your feelings for Jessie have more to do with the how you feel about Shawn. Or maybe you like being appreciated for something other than carpentry skills.*

I pondered these questions as I took my morning runs. The first week of running was painful —an assault on muscles that hadn't been used much. My goal wasn't just to get in better shape. I also wanted to experience that puzzling sensation of calmness and contemplation that occurred as my legs were churning and my heart rate was climbing —a runner's high to replace the alcoholic buzz I was trying to leave behind. I kept the pace slow, trying out different jogging routes, adding distance and elevation changes as I slowly regained fitness.

It was quiet in these early morning hours; the sound of my breathing and footfalls formed a meditative rhythm to accompany the elevated state of awareness I'd been hoping to induce. Without thinking about it, I picked out interesting landmarks along my jogging route, just as I'd done years ago. My eyes would find squirrels' nests in trees, crumbling stone walls extending deep into the woods, and a growing list of repair work that needed to be done on the houses I ran past. Amidst this thrumming of brain cells, I wondered why I'd so willingly stopped doing something that improved my health, appearance, and emotional state.

Of course, I thought about Jessie on these runs. In terms of physical appearance, there were none of the classic feminine features that our society seems to obsess over. She had short hair, a cute face, and a body you'd have to describe as stocky or even muscular, no doubt due to the physical demands of her job. But these traits seemed to be authentic reflections of the self-sufficiency and no-bullshit, tomboyish personality I'd come to know. Yes, I'd seen it before. My affair with Bridget Evans left a mark that wasn't about to disappear. I thought Jessie was beautiful.

Chapter 25

As the Thanksgiving holiday approached, I was feeling more positive than I had since first arriving in Cornwall. I still hadn't had a drink, but I hadn't managed to reinforce my sobriety by attending more AA meetings. I attributed at least part of the successful abstinence to the morning running regimen, which I knew wouldn't happen if I'd been drinking the night before. The other parts were Pete and Jessie, two people I didn't want to disappoint.

My parents were expecting me for the holiday. It would be the first time since my job in Cornwall started that I'd be spending more than a day with them. I knew they were looking forward to it, and I was, too. The last few days before Thanksgiving were busy, mainly because Pete had scheduled the historical society visit for the first week of December. There was still plenty to do before these visitors arrived. Pete had pointed out that showing off a new furnace wouldn't have the same impact as walking into a room that had been restored to its vintage appearance. I'd been concentrating on an upstairs bedroom that had been particularly ugly because of its peeling wallpaper and painted trim. Removing the wallpaper revealed original plaster walls that were structurally sound but full of small cracks that I'd carefully filled and sanded smooth. The room looked much better after wall and ceiling surfaces had been primed and finish-coated.

For the first time in a long time, I found myself getting back into the craft of carpentry –regaining my appreciation for the tools, materials, and techniques required to achieve good results. Instead of stripping the room's painted trim in place, I carefully pried it loose and took each piece to the basement for stripping and refinishing. This work couldn't have been done safely (especially in the confined space of the basement) with old-fashioned, solvent-based products. And my cordless finish nailer made the work of reinstalling the trim go quickly, leaving a tiny hole for each countersunk finish nail that I camouflaged with wood filler. By Wednesday afternoon, all the trim was in –window and door casing, plus baseboards.

I took a couple of photos with my phone and sent them to Pete. He called a few minutes later, while I was putting my tools away. "Sam, the room looks great. I think the commission folks will be pleased," he commented. "Are you heading down to see your parents?"

"Yeah, as soon as I can clean up and lock up," I replied. "How about you? What are you doing for the holiday?"

"Katherine and I are on our way down to Chapel Hill to see my daughter and the grandkids," Pete said. "You actually caught us at a rest stop on Route 78. We probably won't be back till Tuesday, but you can call me if you need to."

"OK, Pete. I hope you have a great visit. And I really appreciate your help," I added. "Not just with the work, I mean…with everything."

Pete knew what I was talking about. "Sure, Sam. Be careful, now. The holiday season is always tough to get through. Go to some meetings if you can."

Chapter 26

"You look better, Sam." Those were the first words Mom said when we stopped hugging. I knew what she meant. There wasn't a scale at my apartment, but I knew that I'd lost some weight. And my drinker's pallor had been replaced by a complexion with more color. "Your dad is out running some errands," Mom advised. "Can I help you bring anything inside?"

"Don't worry about it, Mom," I replied. "I'll just make a couple of trips."

After dumping my stuff in the bedroom, I came downstairs and tried to make myself useful in the kitchen so I could catch up on news with Mom. She filled me in on school stuff, which included a couple of her fellow teachers who had announced plans to retire. "I'm not far behind, Sam," she added. "I'm 58, and I sure don't have the stamina that I used to. Your dad's in the same boat. We want to build up our nest egg a bit more, but we'd also like to do some travelling before we get too old."

I had a huge amount of sympathy for my parents. I didn't know many people who had worked so diligently for so long with so little complaint. They'd dug into their savings to help pay my college tuition, and —so far at least-- I hadn't delivered a very good return on that investment. I also felt guilty for the money they provided when I lost my job and depleted my checking account. At least now I was paying my own bills and slowly accumulating some savings. As for the career plans....well, that was another matter. Seeing the unused collection of dress clothes in my bedroom closet was a painful reminder of the life I wasn't pursuing.

We had a nice, easygoing Thanksgiving. As I peeled potatoes and helped with the meal prep, I resolved to try and eat healthier when I got back to Cornwall. Growing up, I'd learned some good cooking skills from my mom. But the end-of-day alcohol consumption had led me to take the easy way out, making do with frozen meals I could nuke in the microwave.

I hadn't told my parents about the temporary respite from alcohol, and I didn't want to. So, I didn't turn down the wine that went with our Thanksgiving dinner. What a dumb mistake. The yield from the single bottle allotted for our meal gave me just enough alcohol to make the craving kick in. My thirst didn't have to go unsatisfied. Remembering the six beers I'd stowed in the trunk of my car, I made an excuse to go outside, and progressed my condition from mildly buzzed to mildly wasted. Shit.

Chapter 27

The Friday morning after Thanksgiving, I got a call from Johnathan, a classmate from Kirkland I hadn't seen or heard from since we graduated. I'd found out from Grant that he was working in New York, and renting an apartment on the upper east side. "Sam! How the hell are you doing?" Johnathan began. "Are you back with your folks for the holiday?" After I answered, he continued. "Look, I've invited a few friends over this Saturday, and it would be great if you could come, too."

The invitation took me by surprise, and I wasn't sure how to respond. Johnathan didn't do sports in high school; I just knew him from the classes we took together, and because he had come out as gay during my first year at Kirkland. Of course, my parents wanted me to stick around with them, but the chance to socialize with people my own age seemed too good to pass up. Johnathan must have sensed my hesitation, because he filled the pause in our conversation with more encouragement. "Come on, Sam. Get your ass down here so we can all have some fun together." I wrote down Johnathan's address, figured out which train I needed to take, and wondered what I should wear.

I'd like to say that the trip into the city was uneventful, but that wouldn't be honest. I had no trouble finding a parking space in the commuter lot at the Stamford station, and there weren't many passengers on the 5:00 train I took into Grand Central. But I couldn't successfully block the unpleasant memories that came back about my futile trips into the city to find a job, and the numerous episodes of intoxication that often followed. By the time I stepped onto Park Avenue and headed uptown, I had a head-full of insecurities about hanging out with my well-to-do peers. It was the same angst I endured during those high-school parties at the immense, overdone homes of my classmates.

The evening was cold and clear as I took the 20-minute walk up to Johnathan's apartment, mimicking the fast city pace of the pedestrians around me. With bodies covered in winter wardrobes that included not just heavy coats but caps, gloves, hats and scarves, faces were the only flesh I could see. Even, so, I marveled at the variety of ages, expressions, races, and guessed-at nationalities I encountered. I felt certain that most of these strangers had figured out where they belonged, and I envied them.

The crowd I encountered at Johnathan's place included about half-a-dozen high-school classmates, and about the same number of new acquaintances that Johnathan knew from college or work. It was a dense pack of people for a one-bedroom apartment. Without thinking, I gravitated towards the compact bar that Johnathan had set up in a corner of his living room. Yes, I'd completely forgotten my pre-party resolution to avoid alcohol. I had almost finished my first beer when Johnathan grabbed me from behind with a loud "There you are!"

It wasn't difficult to recognize my old classmate, although he definitely looked different. Thinner than he'd been in high school and dressed a bit more boldly than I was used to, in a tight-fitting t-shirt emblazoned with a Rolling Stones logo. He had his partner in tow, and made a quick introduction before switching to catch-up mode. "I hear you're returning to your carpentry roots," he said. This news must have gotten out after Grant's visit. I shrugged my shoulders and must have made a sour face, because Johnathan was quick to add "Sam, I think that's great. Do you have any idea how un-handy our generation is? Even here in the city, I've had people beg me for a good carpenter recommendation."

Was my friend just trying to make me feel better about my inability to get a "real" job? I wasn't sure. But to avoid future discussions of my current state of affairs, I decided to go on the offensive, and keep asking questions as I met different party-goers. My inquisitive initiative uncovered a diverse collection of backgrounds, interests, and professional paths. I found a good-looking couple who were interning for a theatre company, depending on their parents to make up the difference between their living expenses and the paltry salaries they were earning. I met Zeke, a guy about my age who was working at a startup built around outrageously expensive sneakers. The salary was low, but he didn't seem to be worried about money. I also caught up with a few Kirkland alums who were doing different things –working for a nonprofit, taking courses at NYU, or reading scripts for a movie producer.

It was a long way from my life in Cornwall. I couldn't have felt more out of place if I had my tool belt and work boots on. Another failed attempt to fit in. In my nervousness, I'd reverted to an old habit of taking nips of vodka between beers. Two hours in, I was intoxicated enough to start stumbling as I walked around. I needed to sit down, but there were only 2 chairs and a small couch in Johnathan's living room, --all occupied. I stepped into the entry foyer, leaned against the wall, and slid down to the floor. I'm not sure how long I was passed out, but what woke me were the good-byes of departing guests. Yes, there were jokes about the zombie seated in the entryway. I heard a few of these comments before opening my eyes and making an immense effort to get on my feet. It was just after 1:30am. Johnathan urged me to sleep on his couch till morning, but my embarrassment propelled me out the door and onto the street. Stupid move. I managed to find my way back to Grand Central Station, but the next train back to Stamford wasn't scheduled to leave till 6am.

I found my way to one of the cavernous bathrooms on the lower level of the station. That's where I was roused by a policeman a while later. I'd fallen asleep in one of the stalls; the cop woke me up by banging on the door. "C'mon, kid, you can't sleep here," he said. "You gotta go someplace else."

Can you get arrested for drunkenness and vagrancy, I wondered. "Yeah, sorry officer," I offered. "I'm waiting to take a train back to Stamford," I explained.

"OK son, that's fine. But I don't want to find you here when I come back, hear?"

I didn't want to head back outside, but I couldn't think of any other options. So there I was: cold, tired, hungry, and hungover, walking in circles around the historic landmark that I had hoped to be using 5 days a week as I commuted to my dream job in the city. There was a café open on 42nd Street. I stepped inside, got some cash out of the ATM machine, and bought coffee and a sandwich from a cashier who was speaking Spanish over the phone while making my change. It was just after 4am, so I still had a couple of hours to kill before taking the train home.

You've seen the narrow countertops and stools that face the street in these little cafés. That's where I hung out for the next hour, until the night manager told me I had to leave. The same sidewalks that were brimming with people hours earlier were now empty. It was eerily quiet. A big block of contemplative time loomed ahead like dense fog. I didn't want to enter this hazy territory, but it was unavoidable. I wondered how Pete's visit with his daughter was going. I pictured Shawn's happy expression when he saw me waiting for him after school, and I thought about

Jessie's Rosie the Riveter-style sex appeal. That's right, Sam –start off with the good stuff, I reasoned. But it didn't take long for the more critical segment of my psyche to kick in. *How about dealing with the fact that you don't know how to stop drinking once you start? And what's with these fantasies of mingling with the rich and famous? Why keep trying to achieve something that always seems to make you feel awkward, inadequate, and alienated?*

It would be good to share this bit of self-examination with Pete, or my parents, I thought. But it was way too early for a phone call. As I mindlessly scrolled through the contact list on my phone, I found Christina's number. We hadn't spoken in over a year. Thinking back, I remembered that Thanksgiving was a special time for us, because that's when our relationship really became close, physically as well as emotionally. I figured that it would be OK to call, since it would be around the middle of the day in Spain. I wasn't expecting her to pick up, and I wasn't confident about getting clear reception if she did. So, it surprised me to hear her voice come through clearly.

"Sam! Is it you?" she exclaimed. I gave a brief answer, then she continued: "Yes, I remember Thanksgiving. Big turkey and too much food, right?" We laughed together for a moment, then she said: "Your parents, they are well?"

"Yes, they are, Christina. and they still speak fondly of you. How is your mom doing?" I knew that her father had passed away a little over a year ago, close to the time we last talked.

"She's well. My younger brother is still living at home, so he can be a good companion for her. And there is much excitement here, because a grandchild is on the way."

"Wow! Tell me more."

I had guessed the news before Christina shared it. "It's me, Sam. I am married now almost 8 months. Paulo and I are living Barcelona, not far from Javier, my older brother. Our baby is due at the end of February. It will be the first grandchild for my mother. We are laughing because now that this baby is coming, she is taking very good care of herself. More exercise, better meals, we never guessed that a grandchild would make her be so healthy."

"That's wonderful, Christina," I said, trying to imagine the girl I knew in high school as a pregnant woman. "You sound very happy. What does your husband do?"

"He works for a building supply company. Javier has known him a long time, from his construction work. He introduced us, and we liked each other right away, I think. What about you, Sam? What are you doing? Are you happy?"

Nuts. I didn't know how to respond to any of those questions. I knew that Christina deserved honest answers because of the closeness we had shared. But I didn't want to bring her down by talking about the confusion, despair and loneliness I'd been experiencing, not to mention the struggle with alcohol. I didn't realize I'd been silent until Christina said "Sam, are you still there?"

"Yeah, sorry. I was just thinking where to start. Right now, I'm in charge of restoring a historic home in a small town about an hour away from my parents."

"That sounds interesting, Sam, and important, too," Christina responded.

"I guess you could say that," I said. "It's not what I planned to do, though. It's been hard for me to see it that way. I always thought I would get a job in marketing or advertising."

"Yes, I remember you talking about this. But sometimes the things we plan are not the best for us. There's nothing wrong with being a carpenter, Sam. We have this discussion in my family. You have great talent to build and fix things, just like Javier. It's a gift that shouldn't be wasted."

"I appreciate the encouragement, Christina."

"You will figure it out, I'm sure," she said. "Tell me, Sam –Is there someone special in your life? Are you in a relationship?"

"I've met someone, but it's complicated," I answered. I did my best to describe Shawn and Jessie, recounting the events that brought us together, and also acknowledging that I wasn't sure about the chances of developing a closer relationship with Jessie.

"She's had some bad experiences with guys," I explained. "I don't know if she's ready to risk getting close to someone again."

"Have you told her how you feel, Sam?"

"No, I haven't. I guess I'm a little scared, too," I said.

"Sam, if you care for someone, you need to let them know," Christina insisted. "It's normal to be scared when you are falling in love. Are you going to deny yourself this closeness just because you haven't worked everything out in your life?"

The simple answer was yes; that's exactly what I was doing. "It's just that I've made a mess of things lately," I said. "I'm afraid of messing up someone else's life."

"You are a good person, Sam. Don't worry so much. You will be in my prayers."

I knew my phone's battery was running low, so we just talked for a couple more minutes. Christina gave me plenty to think about on the train ride home.

When I got to the Stamford station, there was just enough juice in my phone for a quick call to my parents. I knew that my bloodshot eyes and exhausted appearance would cause some concern, so I promised to give a full report on the party (minus my inebriation and its repercussions) as long as I could head directly to my room for a short nap first. What I really wanted to do was get

back to Cornwall so I could be rested and ready to work on
Monday morning.

Chapter 28

There was a dusting of snow on the ground when I arrived back at Curtis House. I gave Jessie a call to let her know I'd be able to walk Shawn home after school the next day, and to ask about her holiday. "We had Thanksgiving at Luisa's place," Jessie said. "It was nice. We got to meet her two boys, who are in high school. The oldest one –I think his name is Mateo—says he wants to be a carpenter. He would like to meet you."

When Jessie asked about my Thanksgiving, I knew I had a choice: skate smoothly over my misadventures or 'fess up. In the moment before I answered, I thought how disappointed Christina would be if I wasn't honest with someone I cared for. "I got invited to a party in the city," I said. "It didn't go well. I was feeling out of place and awkward. I ended up drinking too much and passing out. It was stupid and embarrassing. I still feel like shit."

"Sorry to hear that," Jessie said. "Get some rest, Sam, and come to the noon AA meeting tomorrow. I'll see you there." Then she hung up.

It was easy to fall asleep that night. Not just because I was exhausted, but also because I'd finally admitted that my determination to control my drinking wasn't working. I needed to do something different. I woke up early Monday morning and resumed the running routine I'd left behind over the holiday. It was slow going, but that didn't bother me as much as it did before. One step at a time.

I spent the rest of the morning doing a variety of tasks to prepare for historical society's visit on Thursday. I was able to stiffen up the shaky newel post at the base of the main stairway by following Pete's advice about accessing the connection from the basement stairway directly below. I did a final cleanup on the upstairs bedroom –one of two interior rooms I'd been able to restore to original condition. And I made a list of the supplies I needed to pick up from the lumber yard in order to keep the work going.

It took me about 15 minutes to drive to the Elks hall for the noon AA meeting. I had time to get a cup of coffee and meet few members before the meeting started. Jessie arrived as Stan, the meeting leader, started to read the opening. When we went around the room for introductions, what I came up with was "Hi, I'm Sam, and I'm pretty sure I'm an alcoholic." Yeah, I couldn't yet make that full leap. I got singled out again when Stan asked if there were any newcomers. I looked over at Jessie as I raised my hand; she smiled and gave me a thumbs up.

As with the first meeting, I noticed some strange language as we read through the 12 steps. Higher power. Personal inventory. Character defects. Making amends. Crosstalk. Some of it made sense, while other stuff was difficult to understand. I smiled when Stan announced the meeting topic: "staying sober over the holidays." Yeah, I already blew that one. But I certainly didn't feel alone when I heard others share their stories.

When I got back to Curtis House, I spent some time cleaning up the basement, just in case the folks from the historical society decided they wanted to see this work area. Then it was time to meet Shawn after school. On our walk to his house, we talked about our favorite parts of Thanksgiving. I told Shawn about seeing my parents and helping my mom make an apple pie. Shawn said "I like turkey and stuffing."

Pete stopped by on Wednesday to look over the project in advance of the historical society's visit. He didn't say much as we walked from room to room, which made me nervous. In fact, most of his comments were about work that still needed to be done. We had a long conversation about whether to restore or replace the original windows, and Pete OK'd my proposal to make some spot repairs in wainscot paneling as an alternative to complete replacement. When we got back to our starting point in the entry foyer, Pete put his hand on my shoulder and said "This looks a lot better than what I saw several weeks ago. You've done well, Sam. I think the committee members will be pleased with this progress."

"Thanks Pete," I said, relieved. "I want to do a good job here, and I'm glad you helped me get back on the right track." I paused for a second, not sure if I wanted to elaborate. Then I continued, awkwardly: "…not just the work issues, but with the personal stuff, too." I went on to recount my drinking binge at Johnathan's party. Then I told Pete about starting to attend AA meetings.

"That's good news, Sam. That first step is the most important one."

"You mean about being powerless over.."

"Yeah, that's right."

The historical society visit went well, probably because Pete led the tour. He did a much better job than I could have of explaining all the repairs that had been made, even including small details like replacing damaged clapboards and making electrical upgrades to the carriage house. I think I did OK answering questions about bathroom fixtures, HVAC upgrades and other details.

The inspection was a good opportunity for me to meet other members of the community. I learned that Carl Patterson, one of the committee members, had retired to Cornwall after working for a big investment firm in the city. Paula Andersen, another member, owned a small shop in town that sold crafts and artwork produced by local artisans. "You should stop by some time," she said, handing me a business card. "You'd be surprised at the talent and artistry in this area –painters, potters, woodworkers, stained glass. We've got a nice selection of items that make great gifts."

Jill Grabowsky, another committee member, asked me if I could replace some damaged clapboards on her house. "I've got a few other repairs that I've been putting off, too," she said. I wrote her name and number down on my notepad, and told her I'd give her a call. Pete had mentioned that I might have folks contacting me about carpentry work. "It's fine to take on these jobs if you do them on weekends," he said.

On Saturday, I took Ms. Andersen up on her offer and stopped by her shop, aptly named "The Artist's Hand." I wanted to get Jessie something for Christmas, but the conventional options didn't seem suitable. I'd never seen her wear jewelry or anything fancy. Something made by a local artisan might be the answer. Ms. Andersen was occupied with other customers, so I had a good amount of time to look around on my own. What I found was a pair of beautiful wooden ladles hand-carved from cherry. The rubbed oil finish really brought out the wood's tawny color, and I loved the gracefully curved handles. I bought both ladles, planning to give the other to my mom.

Chapter 29

In the two weeks before Christmas, I arranged for the floors to be refinished. The contractor –another of Pete's contacts—was willing to squeeze in one final job before the holidays. To prep for floor work, I moved all my tools and supplies to the basement, and moved the old couch –where I'd passed out on a couple of occasions—from the sitting room to the apartment's living room. While the flooring contractor was working upstairs, Pete suggested that I build some storage shelving in the basement. Made from 2x lumber and ¾" plywood, this heavy-duty shelving would hold supplies and some of the home's smaller historical artifacts which were currently stored in a rental facility.

It was good to have the historical society inspection behind me, and to be occupying the last days before Christmas with some basic carpentry that would be less painstaking than the fussy historical restoration I'd been doing upstairs. In my spare time, I cut parts for a couple of bird houses that I planned to give Shawn as a Christmas present. He'd also be getting a John Cena t-shirt from me; I knew that JC was Shawn's favorite professional wrestler. But I thought that Shawn might enjoy assembling the bird houses with me, putting them up in the spring, and watching some birds make new homes.

I found out that Jessie's parents would be coming up on the 24th, so I asked if I could stop by on the 23rd, to drop off a present for Shawn before heading down to spend the holiday with my parents. I didn't want to mention that I also had a gift for her for a couple of reasons. First of all, I knew how leery she was of forming a close relationship with a guy, so I didn't want her to feel any pressure to reciprocate. The other factor was the gift itself –a kitchen implement that a mother might appreciate more than a girlfriend would. Oh well,…

I thought about alcohol a lot during the last week before Christmas. Not surprising, considering that this is the season for overindulgence at holiday parties and family gatherings. I remembered getting loaded at different after-work events and gatherings, waking up the next morning –usually alone but sometimes with another inebriate—with no knowledge of how I'd made my way back home. Looking at these activities through the lens of the AA discussions I'd been hearing, I realized that most of my so-called intimate moments with members of the opposite sex had been fueled by the numbing effects of alcohol. This helped me understand why Jessie reminded me of Bridget Evans. There were certainly similar physical and personality characteristics. But perhaps more importantly, alcohol wasn't involved in these relationships.

When I pulled into Jessie's driveway, I noticed a small Christmas tree in the living room window, decorated with lights and tinsel. I was glad that her parents were coming to visit for a few days. When I complimented her on the tree, she said "I got it from Craig. Do you remember him from the AA meeting?" When I shook my head, she continued: "His family has a small Christmas tree farm. They let you choose the tree you want and cut it yourself."

"That's cool," I said. While we were talking, Shawn ran up and gave me a big hug. I handed over the presents I'd been holding. "Remember, Shawn, you can't open these till Christmas day," I said. Shawn gave me a thumbs-up sign, then went back to watching TV. When he was out of earshot, I told Jessie about the t-shirt and bird houses. Then I awkwardly tried to apologize for her present: "It's not jewelry or a nice sweater," I said. "I haven't seen you all dressed up, so I don't really know what you like."

"Yeah, I don't even know what I like," she said, laughing. "I think I'm kind of a lost cause."

"Jessie, one of the nicest things about you is that you have no idea how beautiful you are."

Hearing those words, Jessie actually stepped back, cocked her head sideways, and gave me a funny look. "C'mon Sam. I'm flat-chested, I don't dress up, I don't use makeup. Hell, it's been a while since I even used a razor. Do you have some kind of dyke conversion fantasy?"

"You're not gay, are you?" I asked.

"No, but it's been a useful rumor."

"It's not that complicated, Jessie," I said. "I just know what looks good to me. I could try to explain how I got this way, but it's a long story."

"I'll bet it is," she said.

"How about I tell you about it over dinner, when I get back here after Christmas?"

"OK, it's a deal."

Chapter 30

The holiday time with my parents didn't start well. I had planned to tell them about my decision to stop drinking, but I couldn't bring myself to do it that first night. So I pretended everything was fine when my mom opened a bottle of wine to go with dinner. After not drinking for just over two weeks, the alcohol did its work quickly. I noticed the look that passed between my parents when I finished the first glass of cabernet and poured a full replacement. But that didn't stop me. I kept drinking and talking during dinner, rationalizing that my improved mood might overshadow the extra wine I was drinking. I recapped the restoration work I'd been doing, the positive feedback from the historical society, and my growing relationships with Jessie and Shawn. There wasn't enough wine to get me drunk, but I solved that problem after my parents went to bed. I finished a bottle of chablis I found in the fridge, and a snort-size bottle of vodka I must have stashed in a back corner of the freezer months ago.

I felt like an idiot when I woke up the next morning. *Why can't I enjoy alcohol like normal people, and be satisfied with a single glass of wine?* I didn't know the answer to that question, and I was sick of disappointing myself and others. My parents were sitting at the kitchen table when I came downstairs. There wouldn't be a better opportunity to apologize, so I took it, sort of. "I'm having a hard time accepting that I can't stop drinking once I start," I said.

My mother's response surprised me. "It's not your fault, Sam," she said.

"Well, that's hard to accept, too."

"Your body reacts differently to alcohol," she continued. "That's what I learned when I attended a workshop on addiction with other teachers a few years ago. If you're an alcoholic, one drink is never enough."

"I guess that's the bottom line I've been trying to avoid," I said.

"Sam, if you want to get help,.." my dad chimed in.

"I've started to go to AA meetings," I said. "I've been listening to other folks share about their drinking problems. It makes me feel better to know I'm not the only one out there."

The next two days with my folks were enjoyable and stress-free. I felt a lot better after coming clean with them, and they were considerate enough not to replenish the booze I'd drunk. I got a call from Jessie the day after Christmas. "Shawn loves his t-shirt," she said. "and I think he's looking forward to putting the bird houses together. I showed him some photos of bird houses online."

I started to respond, but Jessie interrupted. "Sam, I really like the wooden ladle. My mom does, too. She was wondering where you got it."

"That craft shop in town," I answered. "I think it's called The Artist's Hand. There were only two cherry ladles, and I bought the other for my mom. You could stop in and ask whether the carver has more available."

"Maybe we'll do that," Jessie said. "Anyway, it's a really nice gift."

"I'm glad you like it. I'm coming back to Cornwall with my mom's chili recipe. Maybe we could break in the ladle with a fresh batch."

"OK, I'll go with that. I'm sure Shawn will, too. Gotta go. Thanks again, Sam."

After we hung up, I bundled up for an afternoon jog, knowing it would be a slower, more careful exercise because of the icy patches on the road. I know my parents took it as a good sign that I was trying to get back in shape. I did, too. Even though I'd been jogging on a regular basis for a little over a month, I hadn't yet experienced that endorphin-fueled, trance-like contemplative state that used to arrive regularly when I ran in high school and college. But on this day, it returned, an unexpected Christmas gift of revelations that were surprising in their simplicity.

The first one arrived when the exercise playlist on my phone came to a classic Rolling Stones tune. Hundreds of times in the past, I simply let the song's rhythm fuel my strides. But this time for some reason, the words jumped out at me. 'You don't always get what you want, but if you try some time, you find you get what you need.'

Shit. Maybe the implication here is that you don't actually know what's best for you, Sam. Think about it: You chart a path for the career and social standing you want to achieve. Then you stubbornly stick to it, despite the discomfort, bad behavior, and difficulties you encounter. Did you ever think that what you want and what you need might be two different things?

I stopped to turn off the music so I could focus my attention on the inner dialog I was having. Then I started jogging again. All around me, the trees sparkled with meltwater that had frozen during the night, creating a glittering wonderland that made me feel like I was hallucinating. The roads were empty, so the only sounds I heard were icy branches rattling in the wind, along with my breathing and footfalls. I kept running, afraid that this waking dream state would end. About three miles in, another revelation arrived. It was strange but surprisingly helpful that these thoughts presented themselves as if someone was talking to me.

I've got news for you, Sam. There's nothing wrong with being "just" a carpenter. Think about what Christina said –that your craftsmanship is a gift that shouldn't be wasted. There will always be a need and an appreciation for the skills you have.

Despite being sweaty and tired, I didn't want my run to end. It sure would be good to know how Shawn and Jessie would fit into my life, I thought. I knew that it felt good to be around them. But I wasn't sure how serious Jessie was about me, and I never imagined making a family with someone who already had a kid. Before I knew it, I was back at my parents' driveway, breathing hard, bent over, with my hands on my knees. I knew that the running revelations were over, but before going back inside, I wanted one more bit of wisdom. What came to me was this: *Enjoy the beauty and blessings that are right in front of you.*

Chapter 31

In the week between Christmas and New Year's, I was able to get together a couple of times with Pete, who I hadn't seen since the historical society's visit to Curtis House. I left a message letting him know I was planning to be at the Wednesday night AA meeting that took place in the basement of Cornwall's Congregational church. I decided to jog over to the church, since it wasn't too far from Curtis House. Pete's car was in the church parking lot when I got there, and he gave me a nod of recognition as I found a seat just before the meeting leader began the opening. When we went around the room introducing ourselves, I finally found the courage to say the words I'd been avoiding for so long: "Hi, my name is Sam, and I'm an alcoholic."

The meeting was notable in other ways, too. Frank, the speaker, introduced the topic for sharing as "Joy and Tragedy," remarking at the ironic elements in play at this time of year. "It's a time of celebration and joy," he said. "Everybody knows that. But it's also a mine field for an alcoholic, with all the parties and drinking that go on. That's why I always get anxious at this time of year. I don't want to repeat the drunken, out-of-control antics that ruined more than one Christmas."

When Frank finished introducing the topic, I listened as others shared painful memories of holidays marred by alcoholic excesses. Every story was different, and some were more comic than tragic.

But they all had the same trace element. I had my own stories to share, too, but I wasn't yet ready to speak up. After the meeting, I asked Pete if he could talk for a few minutes. He didn't hesitate with his answer. "Sure, Sam. Let me tell Frank that you and I can handle putting away the coffee machine and closing up."

The main reason I wanted to talk was to ask Pete if he'd be my AA sponsor . I'd heard about sponsors in other AA meetings, and in conversations with Jessie. Pete's reply to my request surprised me. All he said was "That depends." I got a longer answer when I asked him what he meant. "I'd be happy to be your sponsor, as long as you're serious about sticking with the program."

"I'm ready, Pete," I answered.

"Well, you're probably starting to understand that AA is not just about not drinking. It's important to keep going to meetings, at least two a week. Do some service by getting here early or staying a little later to clean up, like we're doing now. I can help you work through the 12 steps, like I've helped other sponsees. Are you willing to make this kind of a commitment?"

"Yes, I am, Pete," I said. "Is there anything else I need to do?"

"If you ever get into a situation where you want to take a drink, I want you to call me or someone else in AA."

"I think I can do that," I said.

Pete smiled and said "In that case, Sam, I'd be happy to be your sponsor."

Now about that dinner date with Jessie. When I reminded her about my offer, I wasn't sure that she'd agree to go out with me. But she did, after making sure that Louisa could come stay with Shawn. We thought it would be better to go on a weeknight, when there would be less of a crowd. And given the gossip potential in a small town like Cornwall, we decided to give Greenbrier's a pass. Pete had recommended a restaurant over in Litchfield, so that was the destination. He also expressed some concern about my relationship with Jessie. "She's been through a lot, Sam," he said. "I don't mean to sound like paranoid parent, but what are your intentions? Generally, it's not a good idea to start a serious relationship when you're new to recovery."

Pete had posed the same question I'd been asking myself. "What I know for sure is that I feel really good around them," I said. "Jessie's told me about some of her experiences with guys, so I understand why she's hesitant to get into something serious. I guess the best thing to do is take it slow."

"Good plan. Be good to them, Sam, and take it slow."

When I arrived to pick Jessie up, she came to the door in a snug-fitting pair of pants, a cream-colored sweater mostly hidden beneath a down coat, and a green scarf that matched the color of her eyes. "You look really…nice," I said, hesitating before uttering that last word.

"Having some vocabulary problems?" she asked.

"Well, the last time I called you beautiful, you gave me a hard time."

"True enough," she said.

During the drive to the restaurant, we ended up talking about some of the repairs and upgrades Jessie wanted to do at her place. Like most of the houses in the neighborhood, hers had been built in the 70s –a small ranch with 2-car garage, full basement and cedar shingle siding. It was clear that Jessie had given her renovation plan some serious thought. "The house still has its original windows," she began. "Replacing them would cut our heating bills and make the place a lot more comfortable in the winter."

We discussed other upgrades, too –like a new kitchen and partially finishing the basement. Carpentry topics were a lot easier to talk about than personal stuff, so this made for a comfortable trip. But I hit a snag when we got to the restaurant and the host showed us to our table. There was an awkward silence when the waitress left us alone, after handing us menus and discovering that we wouldn't be ordering wine with dinner.

I looked up at the ceiling and laughed. Then I looked at Jessie. "I was trying to remember the last time I actually went on a date."

"You and me both," she said.

"I'm not that good of a conversationalist," I confessed. "The thing is, it's difficult to talk about stuff.."

"..when you're stone cold sober," Jessie said, finishing my sentence.

"Yeah, that's pretty much what I was trying to say."

Jessie smiled at me. "That's OK. Nobody said it was easy. Not drinking, I mean." She paused for a moment, then said "Well, relationships aren't easy, either. I've learned that the hard way. Hey, I've told you some of my sordid history. You promised to fill in some of the blanks in your background. How about it, Sam?"

I had a tough time getting started, with so little practice in unwinding personal details. But it got easier, thanks in part to interruptions as the waitress explained the evening's specials, took our orders and returned with salad. These pauses helped me to sort out the memories that were bouncing around in my head. I told Jessie about Christina –how we initially bonded because of our outsider status at school, and how the relationship deepened through the fall of my junior year, before a family crisis took her back to Spain.

"So she was your first love?" Jessie asked.

"Yeah, I'd say so. But I had another pretty intense relationship the summer before I went to college."

"Another high school sweetheart?"

"No, about as far away from that as you can get, actually," I said. Then the whole story of my affair with Bridget Evans came out, in a torrent of words that surprised me even as it was happening. Jessie got a jumble of details, not necessarily in the right order: the storm damage that set the stage for my solo work on the pool house project, swimming after jogging at the end of the day, Bridget's broken ankle and its interesting role in our coupling, the bed in her living room where we made love, and other memories of our time together that confused and constrained my ability to find closeness with other women. I'd stuffed this history into a box and locked it tight long ago, with no appreciation of how intense it would be to let it out. My emotions must have been showing, because Jessie reached across the table and squeezed my hand.

"That's quite a story, Sam," she said. "I assume she's still married." When I nodded my head, Jessie asked "Do you still stay in touch?"

"Yes, but things are different now," I said. Then I went on to explain about Bridget's connection to Curtis House, and her recommending me for the restoration job. Jessie lets these details soak in for a few moments before asking me how I felt about Bridget now.

"There's still caring and fondness there," I said. "just because of what happened that summer. But we're both in different places now. The thing that's interesting for me –in a good way, Jessie—is that you remind me a lot of her."

Jessie squinted at me; it was a funny expression, as if she was having trouble seeing. "Is that supposed to be a compliment, Sam? I'm only a couple of years older than you. Bridget could have been your mother."

I laughed. "It's absolutely a compliment, Jessie. Don't beat me up for using the 'B' word again, but you're beautiful in the same way that she was for me. Straight out of the box, without makeup or fancy clothes, you're something special."

Jessie's face got red. "That's nice of you to say, Sam," she said, speaking softly. The body language was telling me she was upset, confusing me.

This time it was me who reached over and grabbed my date's hand. "Compliments are tough for you, I guess."

"No, it's not that," Jessie said. "I'm just so used to being on my own. For a long time now, I've let go of any expectations of a new relationship. I don't have good experiences to look back on, so it's scary for me. And what makes it worse right now is Shawn. He really likes you, Sam. I mean, he hasn't had a father figure to look up to for the longest time. I already know It's going to be devastating for him if you leave."

"OK, I get that, Jessie," I said. "I know what it's like to face things that you didn't anticipate. When I met you just a few months ago, I was desperate to get done with this carpentry project, get out of town, and get my life back on track. I don't feel that way anymore, and that's mostly because of you and Shawn. Look, I just want a chance to get to know you better. Taking things slow is fine for me."

Jessie smiled and nodded her head. "Yeah, let's do that, Sam."

Chapter 32

My sponsorship agreement with Pete gave us both more reasons to spend time together. Neither of us managed to separate discussions about recovery from those associated with Curtis House. This didn't trouble me; there was essential information to be had on both topics. Without Pete's help, it would have taken far longer for me to extract useful meaning and wisdom from the 12 steps. I had no confusion about Step 1 –being powerless over alcohol. I'd proven that over and over. But the self-examination, honesty, and spirituality of the program was arriving more slowly.

When I told Pete about the revelations I'd had while jogging over Christmas, he smiled and said "What I've learned is that a spiritual awakening can come in many different ways. Most often with me, it's as simple as gratitude –just noticing something good or special. It could happen while I'm watching birds at the feeder outside our kitchen window. Sometimes it's just a look that passes between one of my granddaughters and me."

"You mean an awareness of a power far greater than yourself?" I asked.

"Sure," Pete responded. "That's a big part of it. Sometimes it can go beyond gratitude. It might be a tidbit of wisdom or even instruction. Keep going to AA meetings and I think what you'll find is that someone can share something you really need to hear.

I've always thought that when this happens, it's my Higher Power talking to me through someone else's sharing."

"I'll keep that in mind, Pete," I said. "I guess that what I need to do is place more trust in my Higher Power, and be less attached to my own script for how things should work."

Pete just said one word: "Bingo!"

With regard to Curtis House, Pete brought news that my restoration work would need to finish up by the end of March. "The committee wants to hold a reopening in the spring, with all the antique furnishings back in place, and a schedule for folks who want to visit. We're also working out details for renting the house out for special events, like weddings and small corporate get-togethers."

"I'm guessing they won't want me in the apartment once the place is set up for regular visits and special events," I said.

"You're right, Sam. This brings up a couple of details I want to discuss. Let's talk about work first. The historical society has a website, but it's pathetic. We need a new design and a bunch of new content. The committee members are all in agreement on this, and we've set aside some money for the redesign. They know you've got a degree in marketing, and they'd rather give this work to a local expert than an out-of-towner. I'm pretty sure the job's yours if you want it."

Pete was right about the website; I hadn't said anything about it because I didn't want to ruffle any feathers. I told Pete I'd follow up on the opportunity, wondering what it would be like to kick the dust off my web-editing skills and work at a desk again. But Pete wasn't done with the work discussion. What came next shouldn't have surprised me. "Sam, there's plenty of work around here for a good carpenter like you," he said. "I know you've already had folks ask you about home repair jobs. When you get done at Curtis House, you could jump into this market without breaking stride."

Yeah, I'd already been thinking about this, weighing the pros and cons of a return to the business I'd sworn to leave behind. Following Pete's advice would keep me in the area, so that I could be close to Shawn and Jessie. It would also keep my finances healthy, although I'd need to buy a truck and some other tools in order to work effectively as a contractor. Thinking out loud, I mentioned these extra expenses to Pete. I was surprised how quickly he answered.

"Sam, if you want to carry on the noble trade of carpentry, I'd be happy to give you the Dodge," he said. "And I've got a bunch of other gear that I'm not going to use. It's yours if you want it."

"Shit, Pete. I don't know what to say. Are you sure about this?"

"I am, Sam. I'll tell you why. You remember the contractor who took me on when I crashed and burned? Gene Barber. I've told you that AA saved my life. But Gene played a big part, too. He put up with plenty of bullshit while I got sober. He taught me most of what I know about building and remodeling. Then he gave the truck to me when he retired, along with a bunch of tools. I'm paying it forward to you. That's what I need to do. Years from now, I'll bet you do the same."

Chapter 33

The mild winter we were enjoying came to an end the second week in January. New Englanders always pay attention to weather reports at this time of year, so everyone knew a storm was coming. We just didn't know how bad it would be –anything from a little extra shoveling to downed trees and power outages. Curtis House would be less susceptible to power outage, I figured, thanks to the tree pruning that was done in early autumn, and power lines that ran underground from the street to the house.

I did my best to prepare for some shut-in time if snowfall accumulated enough to close the roads. Candles in case of power outage, lots of food, and a last-minute top-up of propane for the heating system and kitchen stove. The snow started to fall around the middle of Tuesday afternoon. During the night, I remember hearing strong wind gusts outside, and the percussion of sleet and snow against the bedroom window. When I woke up Wednesday morning, the wind had died down, and I guessed that about 18" of snow had accumulated. Is there a technical difference between a snowstorm and a blizzard, I wondered? One thing for sure: I'd be getting my aerobic workout from shoveling snow today, not from running. My phone rang as I was heating water for coffee. It was Jessie.

"Sam, do you still have power?" she asked.

"I do. What about you?"

"We're out," she answered. "Not sure when we lost it, but it looks like my neighbors are out, too. I can't see any trees down on power lines from my house, but there are loads of big branches in the yard."

"The wind was blowing pretty hard last night," I said. "So you don't have any heat at your place, right?"

"Yeah, and it's getting pretty cold inside. Shawn and I are bundled up in long underwear and sweaters."

"Why don't you come over here?" I offered. "Or I'll walk to your place and we can walk back here together. Just give me a while to shovel a path to the road so we don't have to trudge through deep snow."

The road had been plowed at some time during the night, but was covered with about 3" of fresh snow when I stepped outside. There would be time to shovel out the driveway later. I got to work shoveling a path to the road from the front door, then made a path to the apartment's door at the back of the house. This 30 minutes of work left me sweating in my heavy clothes. I went inside to cool off for a few minutes, and get a drink of water. Then I put on some dry clothes and headed over to Jessie's place.

Shawn was glad to see me, and when Jessie said "Thanks for coming over," she moved close to me for a second, then pulled back.

"Be careful," I said, smiling. "It looked like you were about to give me a hug."

She just said "shit," then went ahead with the hug. It felt good.

Jessie loaded clothes and toiletries into a couple of backpacks, and we filled a couple of plastic bags with stuff from her fridge. Before leaving, I turned off the main water supply, then opened a few taps to drain water that might otherwise freeze in the pipes. I wasn't sure how long it would take the line crews to clear downed trees and restore power, but the morning newscast led me to believe it could be a few days.

I hadn't given my surroundings much notice on the trip over to Jessie's house. But as we walked together back to Curtis House, I marveled at the pristine beauty of the post-storm landscape. A thick blanket of snow had covered roofs, driveways, and cars, transforming familiar surroundings into a neighborhood of hobbit houses. The faint thrum of a distant generator was the only reminder of modern civilization.

I wasn't sure how we would spend the day, but I was grateful for the company and the electricity at Curtis House. I offered to make coffee when we got back to the apartment, but Jessie asked if she could just rest for a bit. "I didn't sleep that well last night," she said. "The storm was pretty scary, and when the power went out around 10:30, I started stressing out."

"No problem. Shawn and I can just hang out while you get some rest. But the only bed available is in there," I said, pointing to the bedroom. This got me thinking about how we'd work out the sleeping arrangements if these guys spent the night. I figured that Shawn could sack out on the living room couch, while I could make use of the old sofa that I'd moved back into the living room after the floors were refinished.

While Jessie sacked out, I pulled out a beat-up set of checkers that must have been left by the previous tenant. Shawn hadn't played before, but I thought it could be a fun game for us, so it was worth a try. We worked our way through a couple of games, with me explaining the best moves for Shawn to make. He got a kick out of jumping pieces to take them out of play.

Snow accumulation had been a lot less in the southern part of the state. When I called my parents to see how they were doing, my mom reported that only about 8" of snow had fallen. I was glad to hear that they hadn't lost power. Up in Cornwall, the roads were still slick with snow and ice. Schools and businesses were closed. When Jessie woke up, we talked about what to do for the rest of the day. "Why don't I walk down to your place and shovel out the driveway?" I suggested. "You guys can hang out here. It shouldn't take me more than an hour or so."

"I'd come help you," Jessie said, "but I think I better stay here with Shawn."

"No problem," I said, putting my hand on Shawn's shoulder. "Hey, this guy is learning to play checkers. With some practice, he could be pretty good."

"King me!" Shawn said.

I was gone for a bit longer than I thought, mainly because I decided to clear the snow off Jessie's Subaru and pull it into her garage. The weather forecast called for more snow, so it made sense to get the car inside. I found a red plastic toboggan in the garage; it reminded me of days spent slipping and sliding down snow-covered hills when I was a kid. I decided to bring it back to Curtis House, hoping to interest my guests in some outdoor fun.

When I got back to the apartment, it was time to rustle up some lunch. I corralled Jessie and Shawn in front of the fridge, opened both doors, and pointed out the possibilities. We settled on soup and sandwiches for our midday meal, and omelets with toast for dinner. I apologized for the limited selection, but Jessie put my mind at ease. "Hey, we're just glad to have heat, power, and food of any kind," she said.

We spent the afternoon in front of the TV, watching reruns of Seinfeld, along with Shawn's favorite movie –Harry and the Hendersons—and local weather reports. The forecast called for another snowstorm at the end of the week, this time with an accumulation of about 6" in our area. We also learned that it could be several days before power could be restored. This didn't come as a surprise; rural areas like Connecticut's northwest corner usually took a back seat to more densely populated areas when it comes to power restoration.

Just before dark, Jessie and I spent about 30 minutes shoveling out the driveway at Curtis House. I wanted to get at least a start on this clearing work, and Jessie volunteered to lend a hand. "I'm not used to being a couch potato," she said. "The exercise will do me good." We both got a good workout. It was pitch black outside by the time we came in and took off our boots and coats.

After dinner, Shawn insisted that Jessie and I face off in a game of checkers. The contest took longer than I expected, but allowed for some playful ribbing as each of us struggled to balance strategic thinking against impatience. It occurred to me to let Jessie win, but that wasn't necessary; she beat me. Shawn watched the entire game, and was clearly proud of his mom for winning. "Nice game, Mom," he said.

After a double dose of shoveling snow, I was tired and ready to make an early night of it. Jessie helped Shawn get ready for bed, and asked me if I had a t-shirt she could borrow to sleep in. "I think it would be best for Shawn to sleep on the couch in the front room," she said. "If you or I get up early, he can keep sleeping. I don't mind sleeping on the couch here."

"I can't let you do that, Jessie. The bedroom's yours. I'll sack out here. I've done it plenty of times before." Yeah, by passing out, I thought.

I gave Shawn a hug before Jessie went to tuck him in, then turned on the kettle to make some herbal tea, a new beverage I'd been trying out in my efforts to stay sober. I made a cup for Jessie, too –hoping we'd be able to sit down and talk for a few minutes before going to bed. "It's called 'Sleepytime,' I explained, when she got back from putting Shawn to bed. "It's supposed to help you fall asleep. Probably a better choice than the alcohol-based sleeping aid I used to depend on."

Jessie laughed. "Yeah, for sure."

"Do you think Shawn will be OK sleeping in the front room?" I asked.

"I think so," Jessie answered. "He's a heavy sleeper, and he's had the whole day to get comfortable here. Plus, he feels safe around you, Sam. I think he likes it here."

"That's good," I said. "Do you think Shawn knows that he's different from other kids?"

"He didn't used to," Jessie said. "But going to school changed that. I know that he gets frustrated and sad sometimes, knowing that he's different."

"I can sense that, too," I said. "I know it can't compare, but I spent all my high school years feeling like an outsider. It hurts to think of any kid going through that." I realized that I'd started a conversation that was getting emotional and sad, so I tried to change the subject. "Have you ever thought about having another kid?" I asked.

"That's not going to happen," Jessie replied. "After Shawn was born, I got my tubes tied."

"Jesus, Jessie! That's extreme."

"Yeah, I know. Well, I wasn't in good shape mentally after Shawn was born. My parents had moved away, so it was difficult to get their support. My husband couldn't handle having a mentally retarded child who didn't look or act like a normal baby. He actually wanted to give Shawn up for adoption." Jessie paused for a moment, shaking her head. Then she continued: "I was having trouble getting Shawn to nurse properly. I was a mess, Sam, and I couldn't bear the thought of getting pregnant again."

So much for my efforts to lighten the discussion. I felt stupid for my tactless question. I could see that Jessie was close to tears. I got up from the table where we'd been sitting, lifted her up out of her chair and took her into my arms. "I'm so sorry, Jessie," I said, knowing that my apology covered not only my troubling question, but also the loneliness and sorrow attached to Jessie's experience. We just held each other for what felt like a long time without speaking. Then I said "It was a stupid question," and felt Jessie let go of me.

She wiped the tears from her eyes, and said "It's OK, Sam. That's probably a logical question, actually. It's just that I haven't thought about this stuff for a long time." Before I could reply, Jessie gave her head and shoulders a vigorous shake, a gear-changing gesture followed by a loud exclamation. "Whew! I'm going to get ready for bed." She spent a few minutes in the bathroom, then wished me a good night's sleep before entering the bedroom and closing the door.

I was tired and sore from all the day's shoveling. But the difficulty I had in falling asleep wasn't due to the pain in my lower back, or the marginal comfort of the couch. It was hard to put Jessie's story out of my mind. I wondered if her pessimism about finding a new mate had anything to do with the fact that she couldn't have any more children. What I wanted to do was to get into bed and hold her. But I knew that it couldn't be me taking that step. After nearly an hour of sleeplessness, the tea finally started to do its job. Just as I was drifting off, it began to sleet outside. As the icy specks crackled against the living room's window, I heard the bedroom door open. A moment later, Jessie sat down on the edge of the couch. She rested a hand on my chest and I reached out from under the blanket to hold it.

"Do you want to come to bed with me, Sam?"

"Yeah, I do," I said. "Is that what you want, Jessie?" She just nodded her head. I got up and followed her into the bedroom.

Something strange happened when we embraced. I started to cry. Waves of emotion were washing over me –a combination of surprise, gratitude, and relief. Instead of fighting the current, I allowed myself to be swept along. After just a moment, I started to laugh.

"Are you OK?" Jessie asked.

"Yeah, Jessie, I'm sorry. I'm just glad to be here with you. It's been a long journey."

"For both of us," she said. "Now you can kiss me, Sam."

EPILOGUE

(one year later, Wednesday night AA meeting at the Cornwall Congregational Church)

Hi everyone. My name is Sam, and I'm an alcoholic. It's good to be here tonight, and I'm grateful for the opportunity to share some of my story. I'm not sure where to begin. I guess I could start by saying that I was in bad shape when I first arrived in this town. I had a plan for my future: a high-paying job in advertising, a nice home down on the Gold Coast, and lots of parties and social engagements with wealthy friends. Working as a carpenter in Cornwall felt like some sort of punishment, and I had every intention of escaping.

I worked hard to incorporate alcohol into my life. I knew that I wasn't an alcoholic because I never woke up wanting a drink. But once I started drinking in the evening, I didn't want to stop. The thing was, I embraced the drinking culture that went with the fast-paced life I was after. I could always find someone who had more of a problem than I did. Things got worse for me when the advertising agency laid me off. I got arrested and I ran out of money. When I moved back in with my parents, they noticed that I wasn't well.

I took the job at Curtis House to replenish my savings, and to pursue my relationship with alcohol without outside interference. Fortunately for me, my Higher Power put Pete in my path. He shared his story with me, brought me to my first meeting, and agreed to be my sponsor once I realized I needed to make a change in my life. Pete, this meeting isn't long enough for me to describe all the ways you've helped me out. I love you, and I know what you're going to say: The way we repay this kind of help is to help others who are struggling. I'll be happy if I can do that even halfway as well as you have.

Two years ago, I would have laughed at anyone who said I'd be working in a small town up in the northwest corner of Connecticut. But here I am, a full-time carpenter with a growing side business in web design. I found a good place to build a life, where I least expected to. And it's not just me anymore. Shawn and Jessie. I would never have guessed that I'd fall in love with a single mother and a child with special needs. They're the best proof I have that God's plan for me is far better than my own.

I know that there will still be difficulties to face in the future – not just for me, but for each one of us. Let's keep helping each other out, living one day at a time, and believing in a power greater than ourselves.

Made in the USA
Middletown, DE
07 April 2022